Story of

The Haven House

by
Joe Hunt and Amurá Oñaā

Published by

UNLIMITED LLC

2019

Based on the tele series
"The Haven House"
by
Joe Hunt

Other books by Joe Hunt:
Greed Has Friends

Other books by Amurá Oñaā:
The Promise
Amurati
The Seed (Origin of AI)
Johnathan Hood in Close the Door Behind You

ISBN 978-0-578-49582-8

Story of
THE HAVEN HOUSE

Cover Design and Art by Amurá Oñaā

Published by Amurá Unlimited, LLC

I am especially grateful to my partner, Amurá, who has generously given his time and friendship and to our respected peers who supported us on this journey.

Thanks to Nicole who generously gave her time and support to our dreams only to make our valuable venture more meaningful ...

*Thanks, Derrick for your concern and our " jump off."
May we continue moving forward.*

Knock, Knock

The rain came down hard in the city during a late autumn evening. A shadowy figure of a man cautiously races up a fire escape to the fifth floor on the backside of a building, he quietly peeks pass the laced curtains and eases his way into the apartment.

There's a pounding at the front door.

Artie Green jumps out of bed, fearing the worse, scurries around grabbing his clothes and hurriedly heads for the window. Suddenly his lamp is turned on, causing Artie to almost fall to his knees in fright. He then recognizes John Stone, his parole officer, soaked and dripping wet, calmly sitting on the window sill with a .38 in his hand pointed at him. John Stone, mid-thirties, also referred to as Stone sat there drenched.

"Trust me, you don't want to go out there!" he said reaching forward to yank Artie's shirt out of his hands and wipes his face dry with it. He tossed it back to him, "Hello Artie, get yourself dressed."

Artie looks at his wet shirt; he got the urge to say something but knows better. "Officer Stone, I was, I was going to come to see you later on today."

"Sure Artie, that's why I saved you the trip, I was thinking about you back in my office and I noticed the harsh rain out there, so, I said to myself wouldn't be better if I picked Artie up. Quite nice of me, don't you think?"

"I, I can still meet you at your office later on today," Artie stammered.

"No trouble, no trouble a t'all," Stone mimics an Irish brogue. "I'm already here, so now get dressed and let's put these on," he said.

Artie looks at Stone holding out his handcuffs. After putting his clothes on, Artie reluctantly turns around so that he can put the cuffs on him. Stone swings him around and guides him down the hallway, throwing a raincoat over him and placing a cap on him, "Wouldn't want you to get all soaking wet, now would we?"

Someone was still pounding on the door, the whole time. Stone opened the door to see a young twelve-year-old, Italian kid named Vincent Lorenzo, better known as Vinnie.

Stone nods his head at the youth, "How much did I say I'd give you for pounding on Artie's door?"

"Fifteen bills."

"Fifteen bills? I could've sworn it was ten." Stone stared at him.

"Ya know, now that I think of it," Vinnie answered him. "Eh, it might've been twenty,"

"Fifteen it is," Stone said, managing to squeeze out a twisted smile at the little hustler, while slapping fifteen dollars in his hand.

Artie, realizing he had been played, was taken aback by the kid, "Vinnie, how could you?"

"Maybe you'll give me a better tip the next time you have me run an errand for ya!" he snapped back.

"Why you little …" Artie growled.

Vinnie just flipped him his finger and took off.

"Now, now, Artie, no sense raising your blood pressure, he's just like you or me back in the day, just a little better at the game." Stone pushed him forward toward the elevator, "My car's downstairs."

The window was open just enough to let a cold, late autumn breeze squeeze on through, chasing the rays of the early morning sun that were pushing past the worn curtains only to bounce off the dry peeling paint on an old discolored wall.

It floods a secluded room meant for a single person; correction, make that a lonely-single person who just needed a place to stay, a place to crash and dump their failures along with the rest of the old newspapers, beer cans, wine bottles, and jugs. The room like his life is a mess.

In the corner of the room, on a broken-down spring cot, laid a body under a dirty, dingy blanket. Somewhere under the covers a telephone is ringing and continues to ring until the answering machine starts, its John Stone's voice:

"Mister Sizemore, this is Mister Stone, your Parole Officer. You've missed your last three appointments. If you're not in my office by the end of the day, I will have to violate you, with some emphasis on 'violate'

3

and then I'm taking you back to jail. Have a nice day."

After the message ends, the blanket is thrown back and Tyrone Sizemore, fully dressed, jumps out of bed and heads for the bathroom. A wreck of a man, he stares at his reflection in the mirror while huddling over the sink. Tyrone sees a man in his mid-forties, still wearing his crumpled suit from a few days ago; it reeks of two-day-old urine and sewage from lying in the streets. Once an up and coming prominent attorney, He was now a disbarred Criminal Lawyer who thought he could use his gilded tongue to talk himself out of an addictive relationship with crack cocaine, he would have to consider himself lucky if he could mumble a good morning greeting with a neighbor. The face that looked back at him bore the tread marks of a hard street life.

He uncaringly shrugged his shoulders and politely shooed his reflection away as he attempted to squeeze the last remaining bubble out of a small, depleted tube of toothpaste that he smeared onto an old, dry, and used toothbrush, doing his best to get the brush past the film on his teeth. After wasting a few minutes, he poured the remains of a half, warm, open can of beer that had been sitting on the side for God-only-knows-how-long into his mouth and after rinsing, gargling, and spitting, he finally downed what was left.

He re-engaged the image in the mirror quietly hoping, like the character Dorian Gray, for a smidgen of change for the better – nothing.

Then it came to him, the memory of a phone call,

his phone, now where was that phone? He staggered back into the room, stood there looking around for a minute or two. Where, he wondered? He was now a man on a mission.

John Stone puts down the phone and goes over to his file cabinet to pull out a folder. Stone is a man in his mid-thirties, who had been an officer since age twenty. His trail marked four generations of police officers in whose steps he was proud to follow.

Once a highly respected and decorated cop, he had to change his position to a Parole Officer to remain in law enforcement after falling from grace following an altercation where he broke his supervisor's jaw in three places. Determined to stay in law enforcement, he opted for the Department of Parole.

Stone looks up to see his current supervisor, George Frederick, better known as Flick, a stand-up guy in his late fifties, walking down the hall toward him and carrying three envelopes.

"Hey Stone. How's it going?"

"I don't have a clue Frederick, you tell me."

"I got three of your cases here; Thurman wants them off the streets."

"Why don't he pick them up himself?" Stone asked.

"Stone, I'm just doing the job."

"Yeah, I know. Who's on the list?"

Frederick starts looking through the folders.

"Let's see; we have one, Arthur Green, two, Tyrone Sizemore, and three, Carlton Brown. When do I tell him, you're going to pick them up?"

"Tell him I brought Artie Green in yesterday; understand yes…ter…day? I just placed a call to Tyrone Sizemore telling him to come in by the end of the day, or there'll be a warrant put out on him, and I'm looking in Carlton Brown's case folder as we speak," he says holding up a duplicate folder as he stands by the file cabinet. Stone gives a stern look at Frederick and says, "And you can tell him word for word – he needs to sharpen his ass, he's late again as usual because I know how to do my job."

Kirk's Call

In a poorly lit corridor of a somewhat sleazy hotel, Kirk Stone, a young man in his early thirties and an Undercover Narcotics Detective working alone, stares patiently at the receiver in his hand waiting for someone to pick up. Stone comes out of the men's room and walks past his desk to hear the phone ring. He has his coat on and sucks his teeth as he grabs the receiver, "This better be important."

Kirk quickly brings the phone to his ear and covers it with his hand, keeping his voice down, "I just want to tell you I might not make it to the house on Sunday."

"Kirk?"

"Who else would call you with some lame shit like that?"

"What's up? Your voice sounds muffled. Where are you at?"

"I'm following a hunch."

"You're working alone?" Stone questioned his younger brother, sounding concerned.

"I can handle this; it's just some small-time dealer."

"Don't give me that bullshit; if he were that small time, you wouldn't be wasting your time. Now, tell me, what's your play?"

"I'll try and see you Sunday," Kirk answered him, but it wasn't the answer Stone wanted to hear.

"Sunday? Damn it, Kirk, what are you doing? Tell–" Stone yells at him.

Kirk hangs up the phone and heads back to his hotel room.

Stone paces the area around his desk; the office is emptying to go home. He stops, sits on the edge of his desk, angrily slams his fist on it. "Shit!"

Tyrone is racing up a drug-infested block, every so often he ducks in a darkened doorway. Like a lost, stray dog, he watches every person who walks by him. Finally, he notices a few addicts across the street around a man on a bike. Tyrone grins uncontrollably and walks on over; this guy is a dealer who has crack.

"RED TOP, RED TOP, got some RED TOP!" he's yelling like some old-time vendor from a medicine show in the old west.

"How much?" Tyrone asks.

"What, are you new at this? Five dollars."

"Five for twenty?" Tyrone asks hoping to get a freebie deal.

"No, four for twenty," the biker tells him, giving him a look that told him he was unwilling to budge.

Tyrone halfheartedly hands the dealer a crumpled twenty-dollar bill and stares at four vials pushed in his hand, then stuffs the crack in his pocket and hurries up the street. As he's rushing along an old car jumps the curb beside him forcing Tyrone to scurry out of the way at the last second.

"Hey! Watch where you're going!" he yells.

Tyrone notices that no one is paying him any mind about the car incident, not even the driver. He looks down from where he came only to see the dealer still peddling his drugs as new clients were coming to him in a continuous stream, with him calling out, "RED TOP! I got the RED TOP!"

Tyrone looks back at the car; shakes his head disapprovingly and gives them the finger and heads off; he's got his stash, to hell with them.

The car pulls up in front of a hotel with the engine smoking. The occupants turn off the engine and decide to snooze it for an hour or so, waiting for the street to clear of some the of pedestrian traffic and to make sure they're not followed. Pete Pillow, who's in his late forties, is sitting behind the wheel is the first to waken. He's also known as "Yat the Killer" and for having a long-time addiction to cocaine and crack.

He takes a quick scan of the street; there's no one out this late or this early. Yat pulls out a bag of coke from his shirt pocket along with a folded book of matches, takes a huge "bump" up each nostril and leans back. Shortly after, he raps his partner on the chest waking him up. Melvin Knell, another well-known drug addict in his late thirties who would sell his soul for a quality "high," starts shaking his head as he awakens. His face shows the scars from too many years with too long a habit.

"You think he's up there?" Yat asks him.

"Yeah, see the room light? He's up there all right." Melvin told him.

"What are we going to do?"

"Before we do anything, give me a hit."

Yat passes Melvin the cocaine, while Melvin removes a .38 revolver from the glove compartment.

Yat looks at the .38 in his hand, "Man, we should take the whole twenty grand."

"You must be out your fuckin' mind; Victor would have every killer on the east coast after our asses." Melvin snapped back at him.

"I just wanted to know if we're down."

"Wait here and keep the car running," Melvin told him as he jumps out of the car and heads into the hotel.

Upstairs in his hotel room, Kirk stares in a mirror at his tired, bloodshot eyes, he smiles at his unshaven, weathered, beaten face, plays with the fuzz under his chin. He steps back and takes an honest look at himself, pondering if could he pass inspection as a dealer in his own right. On the streets, he's known as Louis Ludlow, an alias that later became Louie Louie (after the song), which pretty much covered his attitude and risk-taking persona. The department knew he was a rogue cop, not one to truly trust a partner after a betrayal that almost made him quit six years ago. They didn't like his procedure; they would continuously read him the riot act for not following police protocol, to work with a partner. Sometimes he would, but most of the time he wouldn't. Kirk loves the rush almost as much as the addicts loved their drugs. As a rogue, he got results better than some units and he felt that's what mattered. After all, he had gotten by worse stakes than this.

He remembers the money belt that's on the cot behind the pillows; he goes over to retrieve it and wraps the belt tightly around his waist. Kirk pulls out his .38, checks to make sure it's loaded and holsters it snugly behind his back. He pulls out his Gold Shield, smiles from some of the fond memories.

Someone's knocking on the door; he stuffs his badge under a pillow, pulls his sweater down over the money belt and surveys the room, making sure everything is in order. Kirk grabs his coat and heads for the door shouting, "Just a minute."

Melvin is standing just outside in the doorway, "Come on Louie Louie, I got a car for us."

After about a twenty-minute ride, Yat eases the car up the street and pulls up on the curb. Kirk looks at the crowded street, considering the time it was more crowded than one would expect.

Yat turns to Melvin, "We're here."

Kirk picks up on an area down the block where everyone is moving fast and looking particularly rough in front of a boarded-up doorway to an apartment building with crack addicts in line buying drugs.

Melvin looks at Kirk before exiting the car, "I should hold the money. Ain't that right Yat?"

"Yeah, I'd give it to Melvin…These guys don't mess around."

"Relax…I got this." Kirk answered him.

"I'm telling you, I know you tough, but these peeps mean business," Melvin stressed the point.

Kirk can see the drug transactions taking place on the street from his car window, leans forward toward Melvin putting on his Madman Louie Louie persona, "To hell with all that! What are we gonna to do?"

Melvin nods and gets out, motioning Kirk to do the same, then leans back in to tell Yat to keep the motor running. Yat nods his head but avoids eye contact with Kirk who comes around the front of the car and heads for the building with Melvin.

Kirk and Melvin walk up the steps to see a burly gunman standing in the doorway; he waves his pistol for Melvin and Kirk to enter the building. At the end of the hall waiting are two guards, the one with a pump shotgun watches Kirk, while the other pats Melvin down. Kirk slides on by showing him the money belt, "It's fat, baby!" he smiles. "Yeah Madman, go on with your bad self," he says laughing and gives him the thumbs up to go on through the open door after Melvin.

Once inside the apartment, Kirk notices two base lamps over in the far corner of the room and there against the wall across from him sat Victor Peters, a short, but stocky man in his thirties counting money behind a desk with one chair on the other side facing him.

Melvin nervously approaches, "Eh, Mister Peters, this is…"

Victor pays him no mind, looking past him and motions to Kirk, "Take a seat, Louie."

Kirk looks at the one chair, seeing nothing else and begins to realize that things aren't exactly going the way he expected, besides Melvin's nervous behavior and the confused reaction wasn't helping matters one bit.

"Do you have another chair?" Melvin asks.

Victor's response was no response. He merely asks Kirk, "How much do you want?"

"I need two keys," Kirk tells him, figuring that it would be better just to follow Victor's lead and keep the transaction between him and Vic; only to have it go south when Melvin says, Victor, him and I are partners…"

Kirk can tell Victor's getting annoyed with this son of a bitch; personally, Kirk just wished Melvin would just shut the fuck up.

Victor asks, "So Louie Louie, what are you going to do with two bags?"

"I've got other peeps in Jersey; they're going to handle things for me."

"Hey Vic, you got anything to drink around here?" Again, it was Melvin, breaking into their business, trying to include himself in the conversation.

Victor takes a heavy sigh, leans over and looking pass Kirk, points to Melvin with a hard-clenched jaw, "You, wait outside!"

Melvin is about to protest when he turns and sees two men enter the room.

The men who entered were Leonard Green, a big man in his 30's, known as "Black Money," a no-nonsense, short-tempered killer and a slim, lean Jayson Peters, around the same age, known as

"Bags, The Collector," formerly an accountant. Upon recognizing them, Melvin quickly works his way out of the room. Kirk turns to see the two men behind him, trying to remain indifferent, he gives them a nod, and they nod back.

"Two keys?" Money asks.

"That's a whole lot of coke," Bags comments.

Kirk turns to face them.

"They're here for the business," Victor assures him.

"Who are they?" Kirk asks though he had an idea, concluding that this was getting a little more involved than he expected. Kirk could tell by the rush he felt even though he remained calm.

Money tosses two kilos on the desk with a thud. Kirk reaches for a kilo, only to see Money's hand on his gun. Kirk removes the money belt as Bags snatches it out his hand, starts counting and then gives a thumbs-up to Victor and Money.

"It's all here," Bags confirms.

"This is that good shit, right?" Kirk asks, sticking a blade and taking a taste on his finger.

"Fuck that, you gonna take a hit?" Money asks him, insisting.

"Nah, I can do that later," Kirk reassures him.

"Do it later? It's good, and that punk-ass Melvin who ran out of here can run you home." Money says looking at Bags who was nodding while taking out his .38 and aiming it at Kirk.

"Who the fuck are you?" Bags yells. Victor gets

up and moves to the side; making sure he was out of the line of fire.

"Yeah, don't nobody buy two kilos and don't test the product, you must be the man..." Money states.

"I just wanna buy some good shit, damn guys," Kirk tries to explain, slowly inching his hand to his weapon.

A woman in a nurse's uniform enters the room, coming from behind Bags. She was Sylvia Papers, known as The Nurse. She has a hypodermic in her hand.

Kirk sees it, goes for his gun, and pulls it out.

"Grab him and hold him down!" she screams.

They grab him, and there's a tussle, Kirk gets one shot off, but it goes into the ceiling.

Victor reaches over the desk and helps hold down Kirk's gun hand, while Bags pushes him back down in the chair and Money tilts Kirk's head to the side as Sylvia comes around and slides the needle deep in his neck, giving him a shot of pure cocaine.

Kirk's eyes begin to roll back; Sylvia places two fingers to her lips, kisses them and then places them on the numb lips of Kirk. "That's right, Louie goes to La La Land," she gives a girlish giggle as Kirk lies dead on the floor; she turns around putting her hand out.

"I do so love my job," she says.

Money looks at Kirk, then at Bags, "Get our two keys and my money."

"I don't have all day," she sighs, impatiently

working her fingers and switching her sweet, can't-wait-all-day ass.

Money nods to Bags, "Give her a stack."

Bags gives Sylvia a bundle of bills, she leans over and kisses Money and strides on out the room leaving all them to watch her ass.

She turns, knowing they're looking and waves at them while walking out, "See you later, babe."

"So, Louie Louie is a narc?" Money wants to know.

"For all, I know maybe, but he's nobody now. What about my split?" Victor says.

Money looked at him hard; he let a possible undercover cop in the house, "You get five grand."

"We agreed on half." Victor corrects him.

Money looks down at Kirk's body and pokes it with his foot 'til it turns over, Money looks back up at Victor. "You can get what he got…" he says reaching for his gun.

Victor nervously sits back in his seat, "Five thousand? I can live with that."

Bags stands to the side waiting for a command from Money.

"Give him his shit." Money tells him.

Bags tosses Victor a bundle of bills on the desk.

"What about the body?" Victor asks.

"Your place; your mess, clean it up." Money looks at Victor waiting for a nod; Victor nods, he and Bags leave.

Grief

A few groups of cops stand around the front desk having some heartfelt conversations, many shaking their heads in disbelief, some trying to console some of their brothers who are openly shedding tears at the loss of a comrade who was not only well-liked but well-loved amongst them. Pain walked through the station like a hidden shadow silently creeping through their midst. The news of Kirk's death echoed throughout the precinct.

Glenn Stone, a decorated detective for twenty-two years and Kirk's oldest brother, sits at his desk in a futile attempt to appear strong in the midst of all the torrential storm of emotions crashing through him. Everyone in the office who walks by can see the news has shattered him; many feel the need to give him his space; they'll talk to him when the opportunity presents itself. He sits there quietly shaking, tears rolling down his eyes. A man in his mid-forties, who is watching the memories of brother Kirk play out in his head, suddenly he experiences a true sense of loneliness. He hears the familiar tone of his brother's voice, the rich laughter they shared between them – knowing he won't hear it again. Finally, he dries his face and works his hand to the phone dreading but understanding his responsibility of notifying family.

Being caught up with the thoughts and emotions of one brother, he knows he must call his other brother – John.

Stone is in his bathrobe, sitting on the edge of his bed, reading through the sport's section of the news.

The phone rings, and he answers, "Hello?"

"It's Glenn…" The voice sounds like Glenn, but not the Glenn he's used to hearing. He immediately could feel that something was wrong.

"Glenn, what is it?" Stone was concerned.

"It's Kirk…" Thinking and preparing to tell his brother was one thing, but now that he heard the words come out of his mouth, it caused him to break, "He's … he's dead."

"Oh God, no! No!" Stone could hear his brother's tone faltering on the other end as he jumps to his feet crumbling the remains of the paper in his hand only to let it fall as his legs weaken causing him to sit back on the bed. "How? When?" he shouts unable to help himself, knowing he needs to be kinder in his response to his brother who's obviously in as much pain as he is, if not more, yet, to be honest with himself, somehow he feared this would happen.

"They found him in an abandoned building, a victim of a drug overdose," Glenn told him, getting a better hold of himself now that he was sounding like he was giving an official report to a fellow officer.

Stone drops the phone and sits on the edge of his bed, he hears something sound coming out of the receiver, leans over to pick up the phone and tells Glenn, "Thanks Glenn, but I need time right now, we'll talk." He hangs up the phone, he thought he heard Glenn saying something, but now was not the time. The world changed on him. Stone leans back on the bed and stares at the ceiling; nothing would be the same he thought.

On the day of the funeral, like the days prior, a difficult sleep nudged Stone into long forgotten memories, some shaded in love, others covered in guilt. Upon waking, he finds himself more tired than when he had gone to bed. John stands and walks over to the window to look out on the streets of the city where he and his brothers grew up. He closed the curtain as his eyes began to tear thinking about Kirk.

Later he finds himself standing in front of the mantle looking at a series of snapshots of Kirk with his brothers in their younger days on the basketball court holding a third-place trophy. There was Glenn, the oldest, himself and Kirk. Stone finishes putting on his dress uniform, but his mind is elsewhere leading his eyes to fall back on the pictures and other awards, he comes to a photo of all of them at his wedding; finally, a picture of Kirk in his Policeman's uniform – a rookie standing proudly alongside his brothers.

John touches up some of the highlights on his outfit and goes to the wall mirror, stands tall in his dress uniform, but he shakes his head at his inability to stop his tears. Man up! He thinks to himself. He holsters his weapon and takes a last look around the room and closes the door.

If anyone had questioned Stone about the services for Kirk, there was little to nothing he would have been able to tell them. The day was a fog, from the moment they carried the wooden casket to Calverton Cemetery.

On the way there, he sat quietly in the family limousine looking at the scenery passing by. Were they moving or was it just life?

Stone didn't know where his wife and children were. Victoria refused to ride in the family limousine, now that both of them were officially separated. She told him she would be there with the kids; she's probably with the new male companion she's been seeing. The death of Kirk, his kid's uncle, was hard on them.

There was a long caravan of police cars that followed them. Victoria and the kids were somewhere in there. Stone really didn't care about his marital and family problems right now. His thoughts raced everywhere and nowhere, all at the same time.

There's a vague moment when he realizes his kids, Samantha and Franklin are standing across from him weeping for the loss of their uncle. Stone knew this was a time when he would have nothing to say to them; for he had nothing to say to himself. Victoria, his soon to be ex-wife was there; her face is hidden behind a black veil, standing behind the kids next to Harold, her new boyfriend.

Next thing Stone knows, he's standing at the open grave site where a priest is mumbling something going in and out of earshot.

"...Kirk Stone, a young man with a promising future, was taken away from his family, the brotherhood of his fellow officers to join his family in Christ and be with the fallen warriors who have given their lives in the protection of our fair city. Kirk is with our Lord and Savior who has embraced him in his loving arms. As Kirk has found peace in Christ, may we also find ... in the name of the Father, the Son, and the Holy Spirit, amen."

Stone and other members of his family approach the casket to toss their flowers on to it. There is the sound of a military-gun salute in the near distance.

John's father, Frank Stone, also a former police officer, watches from his wheelchair and tosses his flower with a trembling hand as the casket's lowered. John's sister, Candice Stone-Butler, also tosses her flower in. She pulls her father's wheelchair back.

Stone's children want to come to him, but Victoria has Harold take them down to their car. She comes up to Stone and in a harsh undertone; she seethes, "This is all your fault, I hope you know that."

John doesn't hear her, doesn't hear much of anything; he comes out of his fog in time to see Candice struggling with their father's wheelchair while her husband, Adam Butler, a Deputy Controller for the Department of Finance, stood there paying no attention to his wife's need. He turns away and begins to walk in the other direction as if to thank someone behind him for being there.

John rushes to his sister's aid, purposely bumps into Adam, causing Adam to curse under his breath only to hear John snap back, "What you say?"

"Oh, nothing, nothing." He could see that John wasn't in the mood.

Stone tells his sister that he'll take his father's wheelchair. He looks back and sees this older brother, Glenn, in his dress uniform, still peering down into the grave opening while tears flow down his face, quietly sobbing. Glenn's wife, Susan, is looking at John for help. She's at a loss at what to do. John turns to Candice, "Hold dad's chair for a second."

Stone goes back to the grave to comfort his brother, motioning to Susan to go back to the limousine while putting his arm around Glenn's shoulder, "Kirk died doing what he loved …"

In a painful whisper, Glenn tells him, "He died for nothing …"

"Glenn, you don't believe that …"

Glenn pulls away from Stone and stares at him, then he turns and rushes down to the limousine to be by himself.

Stone is surprised by Glenn's reaction and stands there, turning to Candice, who waves it off saying, "He needs some time alone."

His father motions him to come on adding, "You ought to know your brother by now, let's go."

As the attendees get in their vehicles and start

pulling away, the ground keepers quickly fill the grave and after a short time, begin work setting the granite headstone which read:

Kirk Stone

June 8, 1952 – March 6, 1983

A New York City Detective

and

Medal of Honor, Vietnam War Veteran

Rest in Peace.

Line Up

The leading headlines of the day focus on the rise in the nation's unemployment, showing long lines, that in some areas wrapped around the block from a few of the offices. Prosperity for the masses no longer was a frequent visitor. People, for the most part, paid little to no attention to the "Help Wanted" signs, showed no concern and made little effort to attend employment offices as hopes and expectations fled under the reality of lack and hardship.

Employment offices struggle as hope and expectations are low under the current blanket of life. Training programs and the city's cutting other public services, and for some people, there is quicker money in the selling of drugs, which unfortunately leads many sellers eventually becoming users.

There are reports of looters running out of stores with an armful of clothes and leather goods. Things are getting so bad that store security is flipping coins on deciding which perpetrator to go after; folks are even robbing drug dealers of their cash, drugs and personal property.

In New York City alone, the number of arrests rises to an all-time high of sixty-nine thousand crimes on the court calendar. Cocaine addiction is on the rise, and no one does a damn thing about decreasing its demand. It is a phenomenon orchestrating felons to sustain its uncontrollable habit.

The Court System considers alternatives other than holding criminals in jail as the prisons are reaching an overcrowding crisis. Incarceration isn't the answer to keep drug offenders from committing a crime. Systematically, jail isn't the solution, and currently, there isn't any intervention to stop the widespread addiction of drug users.

A once proud neighborhood is now reduced to boarded-up storefronts with entire blocks of abandoned buildings. The last rays of daylight spill through the roof of a worn, torn brownstone as six homeless men huddle around a burning oil drum to keep warm.

Outside traffic is bumper to bumper, and as night comes to stand watch over the city, a line begins to form past one of the boarded-up storefronts into a doorway where Money and Bags are serving customers. Money takes the cash while Bags fills the orders.

While Bags passes an order to a customer, he nudges Money, "Something big is happening at the shelter."

Money shrugs his shoulder saying, "Yeah, not sure. The boss is having a meeting tonight?"

Bags was about to answer him when a commotion breaks out a few feet away from them. Some crackhead is counting his singles and won't let anyone pass him; meanwhile, the drug-hungry crowd is growing impatient.

"Count your shit on the side!" yells a woman standing a few people behind him.

Money reaches over and snatches the crumpled bills out of the man's hands, telling him, "Hey dude, you're fucking up my cash flow."

"I wanna make sure I got enough money." he argues, "Give me ten."

Money tells Bags, "Give him nine."

"Hey man, you can't take my money like that …" he barks defiantly.

"Bags, give him eight." Money gives the customer a hard look.

The crackhead sees a gun in Money's belt, says nothing as Bags drops seven bottles in his shaking hands. The crackhead races off.

Bags yells out to the rest of the folks in line, "Have my cash in your hands!"

Bags looks up and sees a young woman in her late twenties who he knows, Bags motions to her, and she works her way through the crowd. Rita Coles approaches him. She's still, an attractive, classy dresser, yet known as a shoplifter, drug dealer and an erotic dancer. Rita also has a reputation for possessing many other talents.

Rita greets him, "Hi, Jayson."

Bags licks his lips, "Hello, Rita …"

Money sees her and asks, "Hey Rita, you lookin' for me?"

"No …Have you seen Tricky?"

"Tricky?" Money scarfs, "As far as I'm concerned,

he better not show his ugly, smart-ass face around here."

Bags is still licking his lips, "Hey Rita, when can I take you out?"

Rita ignores him and turns to see a girlfriend walking up the street. It's Bee, a young woman in her early twenties, but she looks much older. It's hard, but Rita makes an effort to greet her with a smile, considering Bee's ragged condition. Crack hasn't been kind to her. Rita walks up to her, "Hi, Bee …"

Bee gives her the once-over, "Hey Rita; you're lookin' good girl."

"Thanks, Bee, have you seen Tricky?"

"What? You two got something going on?"

Rita sucks her teeth, "Nah, just business."

"Don't let Money hear you say that." Bee pulls her to the side, "Money likes you and hates Tricky."

"I don't want to be that special …"

"You watch yourself girl and be careful. Money's bad news."

They take a walk up the street and Rita is uneasy about leaving her friend with nothing, so she gives Bee a few folded bills. "Get something to eat."

Bee nods her head, "Thanks, Rita."

Bee walks off and disappears into the night. Rita takes a deep breath and shakes her head. She sees Tricky up the block and someone approaching him.

Carlton "Tricky" Brown is in his early thirties, known in the neighborhood as a hustler's hustler. His manner of attire and style would easily fit onto the cover of a GQ Magazine. He's considered in most circles "a lady's man," having a smooth glide to his walk.

"Hey, Tricky," says Tyrone Sizemore, stepping in front of him.

Tricky recognizes the shady, disbarred lawyer with a habit as long as his arm.

"Hey, watch that!" Tricky says, stepping back.

"Tricky, I was looking for you." Tyrone takes a step back as well, not wanting to alarm Tricky.

"You know where to find me," Tricky tells him.

"I heard you're quitting this business."

"Where did you hear that?"

"Is it true?" Tyrone asks him, looking upset.

"I'm thinking about it."

"You can't do that to me, I mean us. You've got the best shit on the street."

"I bet you say that to all the dealers. How much you want?" Tricky is all too familiar with the game; Tyrone is setting him up.

Tyrone begins his puppy-dog whine, "I only buy from you. Today, I'm a little short."

The ol' song and dance, but Tricky knows how to dance, "You're always short. How much?"

"An Eight-Ball."

"How much are you short?" asks Tricky.

"Sixteen dollars …"

"Damn … Your shorts are killing me. Tyrone, you had more money when you were a lawyer. Can you get your job back?"

"I'm working on it …"

"How are you gonna do that, when you're doing this?" Trick hands him a sealed package.

"I'll work something out, thanks. Yeah, thanks." Tyrone bows his heads a few times as he backs away in appreciation, turns and takes off.

Rita had waited for Tyrone to leave and now that he's gone, she races up to Tricky and leaps into his arms giving him a long, deep French-kiss, as he places his hand on her ass.

When she needs to take a breath, she pulls back and tells him, 'Baby, I want you."

"I can feel that …" Tricky says smiling back at her.

"I got something for you," Rita says, pulling a wad of bills from her bra.

Tricky quickly pushes the cash back down, he looks to see who's watching. He catches two desperate looking addicts focusing their eyes on Rita's money. Tricky takes out a .32 revolver.

He tells her, "Rita, you should know better. These dumb asses would rob you and hurt you for a few dollars."

The addicts catch sight of his revolver and race off.

"I'm sorry, Tricky," she apologizes.

"Come on, walk with me." Tricky takes her, and they walk arm in arm up the street.

Red Carpet Affair

Cars pass the tall gates of The Haven Shelter; a retired warehouse converted into a now-defunct Men's Rehabilitation Center.

New and old-style cars move slowly pass an old worn flag that still hangs from a rusty gate. The guests drop off their cars and leave their keys with parking attendants.

It's a "Red Carpet" night for the Who's Who on the streets. It's a night for crime to celebrate its own; to honor those criminals who oil the gears in the city's crime machine.

A custom Cadillac pulls up on the grass. A flashy-dressed pimp, by the name of Charles Maxi and in his late forties gets out of the car. Known as, Max the Pimp, because he lived true to his name and rep, he smiles showing a mouthful of teeth, only to be outdone with over a half-dozen gold chains. He stuffs a few bills in the attendant's hand.

Four fine hoes file out of Maxi's Cadillac; one throws a mink coat over Max's shoulders while two others take each of his arms and lead him toward the shelter. Max sees the cameramen and poses with his stable. There's a barrage of flashes; the cameras are on him.

A sports car pulls up onto the grass. Adam Butler, Stone's brother-in-law, gets out and quickly runs around to open the passenger side door. A well-developed woman, with a pair of breasts aching to push themselves out of her bra, gets out. She's in her mid-thirties, Amy Seal, and for Adam, a part-time girlfriend with benefits.

Adam places a gold necklace around her neck.

She backs her rump into him. "Adam, you truly know how to treat me well," she says, blushing.

"Anything for you," he answers her.

Amy kisses him passionately.

"I'm going to give it to you tonight," she gestures sexually, rubbing her nose against his.

"Well, let's get this night started," he playfully adds, leading her into the building.

A moment later, another limousine pulls up on the grass; a chauffeur gets outs to open the passenger's door, allowing a beefy looking man out. He's Cory "The Beast" Soriano in his late thirties, second Boss in charge of Operations. He is avoided by everyone, who has the sense to know who he is and what he does. Cory has a reputation of being a killer.

A bouncer sees that Cory's collar needs tucking under his jacket and he attempts to adjust it for him. Cory draws a .38 revolver and is about to fire his weapon.

The bouncer jumps back in fright, telling Cory, "Sir, your collar, it's out of place. I was trying to fix it."

Cory regains his composure and apologizes, putting his gun away so the bouncer can adjust his collar. "Sorry about that, I can't be too careful," he says trying to laugh it off, shoving a few folded twenties into the man's hand.

"Thank you, sir …"

Cory looks over and sees a gorgeous woman with her arm in Max's arm. She's one of Max's girls, Dawn Evans, late twenties, a hoe, and part-time dancer. Max has been her pimp since she was fifteen. Dawn sees Cory admiring her low-cut clinging gown and gives him a wink, saying to herself, "This is going to be an interesting night, I can feel it."

She continues holding Max's arm as they enter the building, occasionally peering back at Cory every so often with an alluring smile.

Minutes later a customized limo drives onto the grass. The chauffeur quickly comes around to let out a muscular man known as "Tiny" by his friends. Hugo "Tiny" Barnett, a man, built like a tree, in his late fifties, larger than life and a youthful, fun-loving kind of guy. Tiny is wealthy, and his hands are in every major deal made in the city. He's notorious, and a gangster people have come to fear.

He turns and helps his date out of the limo. Carmen Diaz is in her early 40's, was once a Latin Beauty Queen and former professional dancer. Tonight, she's Tiny's girl. He kisses her playfully; she proudly takes his arm as he leads her toward the building. Tiny sees Cory gives him a nod.

An old Chevy pulls up behind Tony's limo. A

man in an old worn suit and a pair of shoes with a story behind them that spells "Cop." Jim Cannon is a detective, closing in on forty years of serving the force and corrupt for over twenty years, and known as a troubleshooter.

An attendant approaches Cannon, who flashes his badge, causing the man to disappear. Cannon races over to Tiny.

"Tiny, we've got to talk!"

"I told you before; never approach me out in the open like this."

"I only need a moment of your time."

"You want to contact me, call Cory …. I don't want to see you right now."

Cannon appears nervous and says, "Ok, when can I see you?"

"I told you, and I'm not going to tell you again, contact Cory."

Cannon backs away and watches Tiny lead Carmen toward the building.

"You said, this is my time," Carmen says, gently stroking Tiny's cheek.

Tiny gives her an apologetic look. "Tonight, is all yours."

Before entering the building, Tiny notices a taxi coming to screeching halt. The door opens, and out jumps Lloyd Harvey, a man in his late sixties who has been a social worker at the shelter for over thirty years. He walks up to the bouncer yelling, "What the hell are you people doing here? That building is a damn rehabilitation center!"

"Not tonight," the bouncer tells him.

"The Mayor will hear about this!"

"Look, old man. You don't want to cause any trouble."

"This must stop!" Harvey insists.

Tiny motions for Cory to end this. Harvey sees two more bouncers heading his way, with his taxi now gone, he races up the street.

Better Lie, Than Die

It's still dark as Tyrone scurries up the block, looking on the pavement, hoping to find something of value. A female crackhead is bent over in pain, she sees Tyrone and does her best to straighten herself up, smoothing out the wrinkles in her dress, pats her hair and smiles somewhat pathetically at him. "Hi, sweetie, if you treat me right, I'll make it worth your while and be yours all night long." She strokes his worn suit jacket.

Tyrone stares at her dried, cracked lips under the streetlamp and sees the gaps in her discolored teeth. He shakes his head no and runs away from her. Along the way, he runs into Money and Bags.

Bags sees him. "What's your hurry?"

"I, I was looking for you," Tyrone tells him.

Money looks at his partner and snickers, "You know where to find us."

"What did you want?" adds Bags.

"I was hoping to get a little something to tide me over."

Bags starts to giggle, "You look like you already had …"

Tyrone innocently shrugs his shoulders. "It was just a taste."

Money shifts his weight and moves closer to Tyrone saying, "Who did you get it from?"

Tyrone starts to get nervous. "I, I wanted to get it from you …"

"Fuck the bullshit. Where'd you cop?" Money asks him.

Tyrone looks for an escape route. He grows nervous. His mind starts racing, looking for words to cover his ass.

"I didn't buy anything …" he pleads.

Before he can take off, Money grabs him by his collar and yanks Tyrone's face toward his. "Who the fuck do you think we are?"

Tyrone can barely speak; he catches sight of Bags opening his blade. He finally squeals, "I told Tricky to stop selling his shit on your block. Then, he said, 'Fuck Money and Bags, I'm not going to quit. I can sell my shit wherever I want.' That's what he said."

"And you bought his shit?" Bags snapped at him, taking a step closer.

"No, no, no! He gave me a taste. I told him I didn't want it. I only tried it so I could tell you what he did and that's why I was looking for you …" Tyrone told him, hoping it would keep Bags from slicing him, seeing that the blade was now inches away from his throat.

"You're a lying sack of shit," Bags told him.

"No! …I wouldn't lie to you," Tyrone starts begging for his life.

Money looks up the block and back at Tyrone. "Where did he go?"

Tyrone nervously points and tells him, "He went around that corner."

Money releases him, pulls out his revolver and then heads for the corner. Bags puts his blade away, takes out two vials of crack and gives it to Tyrone.

"Take this and get the fuck out of here," he tells him.

Tyrone runs in the other direction and looks back only to see Bags following Money.

Tricky stands in a doorway, on a different street from what Tricky had mentioned to Money and Bags, looking out for any police that might be rolling by. Rita's behind him; she unfolds some cocaine.

As Tricky keeps watch, he hears Rita behind him and thinks about what Tyrone said to him earlier. He decides to tell her, "Rita, I'm thinking about quitting."

Rita hears him but doesn't hear him, "I'm with you, baby. We'll quit together."

Meanwhile, she uses her fingernail to take a "hit," inhaling it deeply. The "blow" works instantly, her eyes open wider than normal. She's short on breath and has trouble breathing.

Tricky tells her, "This is pure, you don't need much."

Rita is swaying behind him and whispers, "Oh baby, this is some good shit."

She takes an even larger scoop, inhales it deeply, causing her breath to become even shorter. She falls into Tricky's arms.

"Shit babe, you took too much …, come on, we got to walk it off.

Tricky walks her up the brownstone, front steps, then down again, repeating the process. Rita pulls away from him, and grabs the railing. "Let me do it," she says staggering. She has difficulty even standing and leans on the railing.

Harvey Lloyd finds it difficult to run at his age. He thought he could get away, but Cory and his boys jumped in their car and took off after him. Harvey race for the corners of the block, hoping the traffic would hold them off. They didn't give a damn about traffic; it only made Cory madder. "Catch that son of a bitch, run him over!"

Harvey turned down the block where Rita and Tricky were.

Speedy, Cory's driver, says, "I got him, Boss …!"

Rita attempts to stand on her own and falls on Tricky, causing both of them to fall in the corner of the doorway.

Tricky tells her, "You should've listened to me." He pulls her up.

Rita struggles to stay on her feet and throws her arms around Tricky's neck. She whispers, "I did, that's why I love you …"

Tricky tries to speak only to have Rita kiss him passionately.

Harvey comes stumbling around the corner. He

works his way over garbage bags, doing his best to hurdle some cans, but he's old, and he's tired out. The limo jumps the curb, Cory gets out of the car, grabs a garbage can top and repeated pounds it on Harvey's head. He screams obscenities as he loudly slams him.

"You won't tell anyone, anything, will you?"

Tricky sees what is happening from the top of the steps and forces himself and Rita back further into the shadow of the doorway, looks over his shoulder, but Rita pushes him out of her way.

"Stop! You're going to kill him!" she screams.

Speedy is beside Cory; he's carrying a lead pipe. One harsh blow, Harvey's body goes limp. He's dead.

Cory sees Rita, pulls out his gun, and fires two shots. He angrily mutters, "Another fuckin' witness!"

Rita grabs Tricky as she begins to fall from the gunshot wounds, and into his arms. Police sirens get closer to their location. Cory has his gun aimed at Tricky's head, but Speedy grabs his arm and pulls him away.

Speedy yells to him, "Cory, come on! We gotta go!"

Cory reluctantly puts his gun in his belt, he watches Tricky all the while, mouthing the words, "You're a dead man!"

Speedy quickly forces Cory back into the limo. "We gotta get out of here!"

The sirens have almost reached them.

Speedy climbs into the limo slams the door and quickly drives off. A police car turns the corner a few yards away. Within minutes, other police cars and ambulances arrive.

While racing away in their car, Speedy looks in his rearview mirror. "We made it out of there just in time."

Cory's still pissed off, asking Speedy, "Who was that guy?"

"Your people on the street would know him." Speedy replies.

Small Talk, Big Demands

The room at the Haven Rehabilitation Shelter is silent with music faintly in the background. Tiny's surrounded by his hand-picked group of City Representative, many of whom would rather not be here this evening, being overly concerned about news of their connections with some of the city's criminal elements being here with them.

Tiny sits at the table, enjoying the view of the men he has in his pocket. It represents power and control, and the wicked smile that sat on his face only displays how comfortable he is holding on to the reins. Seated across from him is 64-year-old, Sidney Lewis, Chairman of the City Council; 61-year-old, Louise Akin, Director of NYC Housing; and Mickey Blondell, who turns 49 today, the NYC Public Advocate Representative. There is also 54-year-old, Martin Waters, who happens to be on the Mayor's Budget Committee; 63-year-old, Gene Halter, Chairman of the NYC Complaint Board and there's Adam Butler, NYC Deputy Controller and John Stone's brother-in-law.

Everyone is finishing up a beautifully catered dinner, waiting to find out why they were brought together, for many of them, particularly the city officials the curiosity was too evident.

Finally, Tiny stands up and speaks, "I want to welcome you all to this meeting. I know that for many of you it is unexpected, but in truth, it has been over two years since last we met with the previous Boss, Raymond "Strong Arm" Samuels."

Mr. Blondell raises his hand.

"Yes, Mr. Blondell?" Tiny asks, being as well-mannered as possible.

"I don't know why you'd invite me. I present no need for you or your organization," Blondell replies.

"Eh, neither do I …?" asked Mr. Halter.

Tiny looks at them both, while he slowly balls his hands into fists. However, he doesn't lose his demeanor. Instead, he tells them with a smile, "You're all mistaken. I want you to work for me now. Since the demise of Strong Arm, records and input into this group have been lacking and somewhat dysfunctional. I feel that many of you have been wandering around in the dark. I'm here to put a stop to that."

"And exactly what is it that I will be doing for you, Mr. Barnett?" Sidney Lewis asks him.

"Yeah, and what could you want from me?" added Mr. Akin.

"Why gentlemen, why the low brows, why do I get such a, how does one say, negative feeling from the crowd? It's simply, you will be doing for me, what it was you did under the leadership of Strong Arm, but with more gusto, more enthusiasm!" Tiny continues as if the meeting was turning into a locker room pep speech. "Why, you'll be working for a better retirement plan."

"Why don't you tell us exactly what you have in mind?" Halter says, standing up and leaning forward with both hands on the table.

"I'm here to offer all of you more for just a little more on your part." Tiny added, smiling back at Halter.

"I still don't get it," Sidney says, shrugging his shoulders and sitting back in his chair.

"Is it property you want?" asks Mr. Akin.

"Yes, I would like to take some over, but that's a start; only a start. The rest of my needs will I will give to some of you on a need to know basis," Tiny offered.

"What do you need to use it for, taxes?" Mr. Lewis questions.

"He wants to use the mainstream property that is available, at least that's the impression I'm getting," Adam Butler says, offering an opinion.

Tony sees Cory returning from the task he sent him on. He steps back from the table and waits until Cory reaches him. "What about our noise?" he asks.

"It died down," Cory smiles at him.

Tiny turns back to his guests and tells them, "Gentlemen, Cory will be the person whom you'll contact should you need any specifics details. He will also let you know about some of the specific changes that I may require of you in the future."

"Wait a second now. How do we build on our retirement plan?" Mr. Blondell demands, wanting an answer.

All of them watch Tiny turn and walk out.

"What the hell was that all about?" Mr. Halter inquires.

Cory is already getting a little upset with the questions, and he just got there.

"It's about retirement and insurance," Cory answers, not displaying the level of control Tiny had.

"Insurance, what hell insurance do you mean?" Halter asks, forgetting to whom he was talking.

Cory gets up and walks over to where Mr. Halter is sitting, yanks him out of his seats and plants a hard-right fist into his gut, causing Halter to fold over onto the floor. "It's the kind of insurance that allows you to reach the age of retirement. Understand?" he states standing over Mr. Halter. Cory looks at the rest of them, "Understand?" The rest nodded their heads.

He helps Halter back into his seat and tells all of them in a stern voice, "Any questions, direct them to me."

Mr. Akin gets up and tells them that he'll meet with them individually.

Upon getting up to go, Sidney Lewis, says under his breath, "Is that it? We come to a meeting, a meeting about the same bullshit more or less."

Cory caught part of his dribble and looked at him saying, "Make the best of it …"

Lewis sheepishly nods.

Shelly's Moves

Detectives and parole officers have their badges exposed as they walk past the security desk. People are locked in conversations covering a myriad of topics. The voices loom from hot and heavy to friendly chit-chat. Meanwhile, law enforcement personnel wait impatiently on their elevator. When one finally opens up on the ground floor, they charge forward like a herd of cattle.

An elevator car is full, and the doors start closing; those watching from the outside decide that there are enough people on it, but just before it closes, a hand plops through forcing the doors to open. In jumps Parole Officer, Shelly West, an attractive young woman in her mid-thirties who has been on the job for about eleven years. She's a joyful soul who people love to be around.

Shelly cheerfully greets them with a smile, "Morning, everyone!"

"Good morning," a few of them respond. Shelly squeezes in close to a colleague by the name of Russell Allen, a bitter, frustrated 52-year-old parole officer. She begins reading the newspaper he's reading. He attempts to avoid her prying eyes by shifting his newspaper.

"Let me guess," Russell says to her, partially

45

closing the paper in disgust, "You didn't buy a paper again. Right?"

"I didn't have the time …" Shelly explains, flirting shyly, softly reopening the page he was on.

She places her hand on the paper and keeps him from turning the page while she continues reading.

He looks at her with a "what the fuck!" expression saying, "There's a newsstand in the lobby …:

She giggles girlishly saying, "I only had a minute to get upstairs."

Shelly reads a headline "A Stray Bullet Kills Young Girl." She shakes her head commenting, "Another drug-related shooting …"

Russell turns back to the article she read from saying, "I don't remember it saying any mention of drugs."

The elevator door opens, Russell is carefully going over the item as Shelly exits. He yells to her, "I still don't see it …"

She walks away and answers him, "You will." And then adds just as quickly, under her breath, "One day." The elevator door closes on Russell's confused face.

On the floor, Shelly notices some parolees are early. She walks up to the security desk and meets Officer Charles Newton.

"Morning, Officer Newton, this bunch is early."

"Good morning. Officer West. Yeah, so I noticed, any of them yours?"

"Not that I can tell," she answers him, "How was your vacation?"

Without displaying any emotions, he matter-of-factly says, "Paris was nice."

Shelly put her hands on her hips; her body language questioning his tone of voice as she responds, "You didn't have a good time."

Newton broke into a smile from her attitude. "My wife had a wonderful time using up all our credit cards."

Shelly shakes her head and signs into the logbook. She walks on down the hall until she reaches Parole Officer Stone's office.

She checks herself to make sure she didn't misplace any of her beauty on the way up. Stone had taken a leave of absence after the death of his brother; Kirk and it's been a week since she saw him last. They talked on the phone the night before, but she didn't want to express her feelings about Kirk on the phone. She stands outside his door and takes a breath, hoping he's inside. She taps and opens the door to see him sitting behind his desk.

Stone is on the phone; Shelly stands in the doorway. They both smile at each other, and he beckons her to come in and take a seat.

She covers her heart and says, "I'm so sorry for your loss. I would've said something at the funeral, but I didn't know if it was the proper thing to do at that time."

Stone's nod assures her that it was okay. He places his hand over the receiver,

Shelly whispers, "Are we on for tonight?"

"Sure thing," Stone answers.

Shelly quietly gets up, giving the signal to remain seated. "You're working; we'll talk later." She blows him a kiss and leaves.

Stone goes back to his conversation, leans back and glances at the family photos on his desk — the photo of his soon to be ex-wife, Jennifer Stone, an attractive 34-year-old woman; his eleven-year-old daughter, Samantha and his nine-year-old son, Franklin, who reminds him of himself in his younger days. He can understand Jennifer's action, but he tenses up at the thought of having less contact with his children.

The voice on the phone snaps him back into the conversation. It was Thurman on the other line saying, "You just can't feel sorry for them!"

"Sir, I don't feel sorry …"

"Listen, they understand jail. Put them there."

The door opens and Zeke Childs, Stone's childhood friend, and partner for the last eleven years walks in. Zeke has been a parole officer for more than seventeen years. He sits down near the corner of Stone's desk and looks at the open folder. He was also at Kirk's funeral, but he had no intention of bringing up the subject unless Stone did.

Stone is still talking to Thurman; he moves the folder out of Zeke's reach. "Sir, my job is more than just putting people in jail."

Before closing the folder, he rereads the top sheet: "Parole Violation," the word "Warrant" is underlined in red. The name on the folder is Carlton Brown –

AKA "Tricky." Convicted for possession with intent to sell to undercover officers, sentenced to five years at Comstock Correctional Facility, Great Meadow, New York. Time served: 4 years, two months. Known to carry a .32 revolver.

Thurman orders him, "Let the courts put them where they belong!"

Stone fires back, "I know my job, sir!"

"Then perhaps you'd be happier doing a different job, somewhere else," Thurman strongly suggests.

"That's something I'd like to take under consideration. Thank you, sir," Stone answers, abruptly ending their discussion with a "click."

"Did you just hang up on Director Thurman?" Zeke asks, somewhat surprised, but offering a demented smile.

"He's a bureaucratic ass ..." Stone says, throwing up his hands.

"What's up with Mr. Brown, is he up for review?"

"Nah, he just hasn't reported in, in over a month," Stone tells him.

"Are we to pay him a visit today," Zeke questions Stone.

"I don't know," Stone sighs, "maybe later. I'm giving him a chance to report."

"Well then, please don't call too early, we don't want to disturb the wife," Zeke says, smirking as he leaves the office.

Uninvited

The light from the television set casts shadowy images dancing across the ceiling of a darkened apartment. From a curled-up figure on a couch, booms loud snoring, loud enough to wake the sleeper. Tricky jumps up wondering what or who is making that noise.

He rocks in his seat, looking around in the dark. His vision is blurry, but slowly begins to clear, coming into focus on a half-filled bottle of vodka; he downs a few gulps. It occurs to him that there's a bowl of cocaine on the table as well.

Tricky sees the red light on his answering machine flashing, indicating a call's coming in. However, he's fixated on reaching the cocaine; inhales a huge amount. He oozes back into the couch; closes his eyes and ready's himself to be consumed by the cocaine.

He suddenly hears movement outside in the hall; someone is knocking on his neighbor's door. Tricky's on edge and reaches for his gun on the table, accidentally starting his answering machine.

He first hears his voice, "Hi, I'm not available, but if you leave your name and number, I will get to you."

The message starts: "Hi, baby, it's Rita, I've got something for you."

It goes off, and a new message begins: "Mr. Brown, this is Parole Officer Stone. You missed your last four appointments. If you are not in my office by 5 pm, you'll violate your parole; a warrant will be issued against you."

By the time the message ends Tricky is fast asleep.

A car is slowly moving up the block; Speedy is driving it, and he's scanning the numbers above every building doorway. Beside him is Cory's bodyguard, Lester who takes out a folded piece of paper. "We're looking for 1311; he's in apartment 3A," he says, reading the note.

Cory rises from the back seat. The car pulls to a stop, Speedy says, pointing, "1311, we're here."

Cory pulls a gun from his waist jumps out of the car; he looks to make sure the coast is clear and enter the building with Lester following him.

Tricky's sleep is interrupted by his choking; he jumps up grabbing the bottle of vodka, while accidentally knocking his gun behind a pillow on the sofa. He goes for more cocaine, and it doesn't take long to start working on him. He falls back and starts to drift off.

Tricky's doorknob slowly begins to turn, then stops. All of a sudden, the door flies off the hinges. Tricky's eyes pop wide open; Tricky gets up on his feet. Lester charges into the dark apartment; rushes over to Tricky and grabs him by the throat. Cory eases into the room nonchalantly, watches Lester slowly choking the life out of him.

"Don't kill him yet," Cory tells him.

Lester tosses Tricky back onto the couch.

"Come on, Boss. Let me do him in …" Lester pleads.

Cory confidently moves around the room looking the place over in the dark. "You're gonna die, just like your bitch, because you saw us. I'm thinkin' how we should get rid of your ass."

"Let me throw the son of a bitch out the window," Lester yells.

Lester goes over to Tricky and grabs him by the throat again. As he tries to lift Tricky off the couch, Tricky's fingers frantically search behind the couch pillow and locating the handle of his gun; he's able to push the nozzle under Lester's chin. Two quick shots slam into Lester's throat, causing him to fall back, while releasing Tricky. Lester crashes into the table. Cory gets some of the blood sprayed on him as he stares at the blood gushing from Lester's neck.

Lester desperately tries to breathe while trying to catch his breath at the same time. He struggles with the wound on the floor; suddenly, he stops breathing. He's dead.

Cory's jarred out of his trance; sees Tricky about to get up; he kicks the gun out of Tricky's hand, sending him flying across the floor. Tricky feels along the floor; a nail file falls into his fingers. He sees Cory advancing toward him with a gun aimed at his head.

"Damn you; your drug-dealing days are over!"

Tricky silently watches him and waits. Cory draws closer cocking the hammer.

Tricky knocks the gun away from his face and lunges forward with the nail file. It goes straight into Cory's left eye. Cory screams out in pain as the nail file lodges in deep. He stumbles forward, trips over Lester's body and hits his head against another piece of furniture. He's out cold.

Tricky struggles to get up; he backs out of the apartment and takes off. A few curious neighbors are sticking their heads out of some apartments trying to figure out who's making the racket, only to pop their heads back in when they see Tricky backing into the hallway. He hurries out the building and races down the block and around the corner.

Speedy is leaning back in the car seat when he sees a figure race out of the building and runs down the block, only to disappear. He gets out of the car trying to figure out what might've happened, then races into the building. When he gets near the third floor, he draws his gun, slithers down the hall to see a door off the hinges with only the light from the hallway offering some visibility.

"Boss, you in there?" he calls.

Speedy steps further into the room, as his eyes adjust, he's startled at the sight of Lester's body covered with blood.

He gets frightened. "Lester!"

53

Speedy stares at the dead body. There's a moan coming from the back of the couch; Speedy eases around Lester's body only to see Cory struggling to get up. There's blood all over Cory's face; Speedy sees the nail file buried in his eye. Cory moans even louder. Speedy helps him to his feet.

"Wait a minute, Boss. Let me pull it out," he tells Cory.

"No! Then the bleeding won't stop," Cory tells him.

"Let me see what I can find." Speedy searches the apartment.

"Hurry up! I got to see a doctor," Corky barks. He has a hard time keeping his balance; Speedy rushes back with a towel.

"This is all I could find," Speedy tells Cory.

Speedy puts the towel under Cory's eye and leads him toward the door. At the door, Cory remembers his gun. He turns pointing around the room and tells Speedy to get his gun, "My gun, it's over there on the floor."

Speedy runs back into the room and picks up the first gun he sees, shoving it into his pocket. It happens to be Tricky's gun.

"I got it," he says, getting back to Cory.

"Get Chuck to clean up this mess."

"I'll call The Cleaner after you see a doctor," Speedy tells him.

Speedy escorts Cory out of the building; gets him in the car and drives off.

Cory grabs Speedy by the arm, demanding of Speedy, "Take me to Scissers, our upstate Doc. I don't want anyone to know that some two-timing, drug-pushing, asshole punk did this to me. Do you hear me, tell no one, not even the boss."

"Yeah, yeah, sure, Cory, sure," Speedy utters, not wanting to get on Cory's bad side.

Town Hall Talks

Camera crews are everywhere focusing on the group on the stage.

The City's elite pack Town Hall. It's early afternoon, and New York Law Enforcement representatives sit on the Town Hall stage. Among them sat two deputies from the Mayor's Office and two detectives from the New York City Police Department.

A newscaster straightens his tie and positions himself in front of a station camera. It's Harmon Palmer, in his early forties. He used to be one of the top networks newscasters, but drinking became a permanent dance partner in his life, leading to the demise of his career on a major network. Drinking also edged his wife out of the picture, leaving them divorce.

Now he's a street reporter for Access Cable Television.

He smooths out his hair and assumes his position, "Hi, I'm Harmon Palmer, and good evening. We're live at Town Hall, and the meeting between city officials and the Neighborhood Task Force is about to begin."

Off to his side, a gathering crowd grows restless. Police officers begin stationing themselves at every door.

A voice in the crowd yells out, "Our neighborhoods aren't safe anymore!"

On the stage, the Chairman of the City Council, Jimmy Lewis, bunkered down in his late sixties and well-past his retirement, which should've been some years ago, rises from his seat and goes over to the podium. With frustration etched in his wrinkled face, he scans the audience. Jimmy was never one to handle a disagreeable situation well. When dealing with him, he'd remind people of an outdated 8-track player, because now and then, he'd get stuck.

Jimmy starts tapping the mic at the podium. He grows angry with the crowd, "Order! You people need to come to order!"

A Deputy Mayor in her late thirties, Wanda Wilder, is amazed at the amount of confusion displayed from not only those in the audience but those on the stage. She turns to her colleague, a well-known Deputy Mayor and says, "Are you sure you want to do this?"

A tall, handsome man gets up; he's Senior Deputy Mayor Dr. Leo Fairgood, a probable candidate for the next Mayoral election. In his forties, he's respected and admired by voters, who refer to him as "Doctor Fair."

As he quietly approaches the podium, Dr. Fairgood says to himself, "This has gotten out of hand."

Jimmy Lewis is losing control, repeatedly hits the microphone only to cause the crowds to hurl insults at him.

He yells back, "You people need to shut the hell up!"

Leo steps in and takes the microphone from Jimmy; the crowd cheers for Leo as most of the audience recognizes him.

Leo raises his hand to calm down the audience, "Please, please come to order! I am here because the Mayor has heard your concerns. We want to help."

The noise slowly settles down; the people begin to listen.

A citizen raises his hand, and Leo directs that he speak from one of the podiums set up in the aisles.

A senior woman approaches the mic and asks, "What about getting rid of the drugs in our neighborhood?"

"Yes, let's take our neighborhood back," Fairgood answers her.

"And how do we do that?" came a voice from the front.

"Well, most of the drug users live in the neighborhood. Am I correct?" Leo responds.

The senior woman responded from the aisle podium, "Yes, we know most of them, not by name, but we know them." Many in the audience confirm her statement by nodding or yelling an affirmation.

A front row citizen yells out, "Those people are criminals!"

Another yells out, without waiting to be escorted to an aisle podium, "The streets offer nothing but trouble, I've been robbed three times by the same guy." Others affirm his statement.

The senior woman at the podium raises her hand

and asks, "What do we with them? How do we solve this problem?"

"We start with them," Fairwood answers, raising his hands to calm some of the folks he senses are uncomfortable with his answer, "We start with them because, without their drug use, there'd be no need for the dealers."

"And just how do we get the drug users to stop using drugs?" came another voice.

Using his political "assure the people voice," he answers, "We'd provide them with other options, wherein we offer them a jail sentence or a drug treatment program."

A person at the other aisle podium questions him, "And where would they get this so-called treatment?"

"Why, in our rehabilitation shelter," Fairgood tells him.

"Where, at that Haven Shelter?" he asks.

"That 's the ideal place for their drug treatment," Fairgood responds.

"Oh no! Not that place!" the senior woman protests, along with many other objecting voices in the audience.

From behind a pillar in the rear of the auditorium, Tyrone watches the proceedings. A police officer at an exit door sees him and turns to his partner, "Hey, is that the Sizemore guy?"

"Who, the lawyer?" queries his partner.

Tyrone realizes he's been recognized, avoids making eye contact and hurries out of the building.

The cop who initially saw him says, "Now, I wonder why he's here?"

A few people in the audience are up on their feet, becoming very vocal, "Why, you can't walk near the place;" "those people wait for you to get your check;" "you get beat up and end up in the hospital!"

The control that was settling in at one time was slowly losing its grip in the hall.

"You could press charges against them," Fairgood offers them.

"That's easy for you to say! You got the police and the Mayor behind you," came a shout.

"I haven't always had the police on my side or worked for the Mayor. I come from this neighborhood as well," Fairgood says, reconnecting his ties to the audience.

"Yeah, but you don't live here anymore!" echo a few voices.

"I still have friends that live here in the neighborhood and this district," he humbly confesses.

"But what happens when we get a visit from one of those tough guy's friends?" came a shout.

Murmurs of concern began circling throughout the audience.

Dr. Fairgood tries to regain the control he initiated, "We'd arrest them."

"That shelter should be burnt down!" came a shout followed by cheers and affirmations.

"No, we need to rebuild our neighborhood, not burn it down," Fairgood attempts to regain some trust from his constituents.

"Moving these people in our community won't help anything," someone else shouted.

"I'm willing to sit with some of you, as I've always done in the past and listen to grievances so we can iron out any differences. Come on people, work with me. We can do it together!" Fairgood sincerely tells them.

After a few more positive quotes, Leo does what he's known for, he brings out the best in them. He has them cheering and applauding.

Eric Stevens, a cop for over twenty years, an alcoholic, known to have a temper and who hates all people of color, whispers to his partner, Cannon, "Look at all these suckers, they think things will change."

Cannon shrugs his shoulders as if he gives a damn.

Dr. Fairgood is finishing up his time with the audience, things are on an upbeat note, and he's smart enough to know to leave when the going gets good. He waves to his constituents and says, "Thank you, thank you. Now we have two of our finest New York City Detectives here with us tonight."

Not paying attention to what's going on, Eric continues feeding Cannon his opinions, "What a bunch of fools…"

Fairgood waves one last time casting his hand over to introduce Eric and Cannon, "Now let's welcome our New York City Detectives."

Cannon and Eric get caught off-guard; they did not expect to speak at this meeting. Both of them stand, but Eric decides to take his seat, telling Cannon, "It's your show."

Cannon's peeved that Eric left him holding the bag, he mustards up some strength and nervously approaches the podium. The silence of a distrusting crowd greets him.

"We've heard your concerns, and we are working on them," Cannon says, doing his best to wing it.

A citizen at the podium to his right asks, "What are your plans to make us feel safe?"

"We scheduled more police cars to patrol your streets so that you will feel safer."

"Yeah?" screams another citizen, "Well, what about the damn shelter? That's the main problem."

"We assure you, we have that place under our radar." Cannon answers him.

His response doesn't appear to satisfy some of the onlookers as another yells out, "When are you going to close that place down?"

"Eh, I'm currently not at liberty to share any of our strategies with you at this time, but you will be informed when things happen. I want to thank you for your questions," Cannon says seeking to rid himself of this experience; Cannon waves and returns to his seat, leaving the crowd in silence.

When he sits down, Eric leans over and whispers, "Good job."

Cannon, however, is somewhat confused and asks Eric, "Where's this place they're talking about?"

Spot Check

It's early morning, and the sun has yet to rise. Stone is not alone in front of Tricky's door. Zeke's on one side, and Shelly's on the other side checking her revolver. Stone is up against the door, listening. A gang of policemen in riot gear is behind him. Everyone is waiting for his signal.

"I don't hear anything," Stone tells them.

"You want us to knock?" Shelly asks him.

"Do we need an invitation?" Zeke asks both of them.

Shelly grabs Stone and pulls him out of the way. She has her 9mm drawn and kicks the door open; she races in the apartment and lays against the wall.

She yells, "Clear!"

Stone follows in with Zeke behind him. Stone waits in the living room as the Riot Squad goes past him, toward the back room. Sunlight begins to filter into the apartment.

They shout, "Clear!"

Stone hesitates before going any further. He notices the rug has one cleaner surface area than other parts of the rug.

"You good here?" asks Zeke who's watching Stone.

Stone nods and looks around the room. Zeke goes into another room. Stone looks back at the door to the apartment and notices recently added hinges used to cover up a broken door fixed before their arrival.

He spots a shell casing embedded in the corner of the rug. He starts to go behind the sofa where it's still dark, takes out his flashlight and in a far corner, covered by a full-length curtain is a blood-stained revolver. He bags as evidence.

Stone hears movement outside the hall and slowly draws his weapon. Cannon and Evans enter. They're startled seeing Stone's gun pointed at them.

"Why are you here?" Stone asks, still holding his gun.

"We're looking for Carlton Brown," Eric tells him.

Cannon appears nervous, telling Stone, "Could you put that gun away?"

"Why you here?" Stone is not yet satisfied with their answer.

"Someone saw him over on Prospect, where a witness got shot," Cannon tells him.

"Is he the suspect?" Stone asks.

Eric begins to get uneasy as well. "We just want to ask him a few questions."

"Is he a witness?" Stone questions.

"Not exactly," Cannon says.

"What do you mean, not exactly?" Stone looks at them.

Eric steps up and says, "We should be asking the questions."

Stone still has his gun on them, "Not from where I see it."

Cannon doesn't know how to sway Stone to his point of view and finally pleads for a calmer approach, "Stone, put that thing away. Alright?"

Shelly rushes back into the room, sees the two detectives. Stone decides to holster his revolver.

Shelly gets curious; she can feel there's tension amongst the three of them. She gives them the once over and decides to question the two detectives, "Why are you two here?"

"We came to see Mister Brown," Cannon answers her.

Shelly shifts her stance, placing her hands on her hips, "Why?"

Eric dismisses her attitude and tells her, "He might be involved in a shooting."

"And who told you that?" Stone questions him.

"You know those people talk …" Eric explains.

"What people?" Stone quickly snaps at him.

"The people in this neighborhood," says Eric.

Shelly moves in a little closer, almost too close and snarls, "The people in this neighborhood wouldn't talk to the likes of you!"

Eric takes a defensive step back, "I resent that."

Stone knows that Shelly can easily get into "storm" mode; he calmly tells Evans and Cannon, "You guys really don't' have a reason to be here."

Cannon and Evans see Morris and his squad as they come out from a back room. Morris stops when he reaches Stone. "If you don't need us, we'll check out."

Eric starts to feel uneasy at what he sees. "Who authorized all of this?"

Stone dismisses Eric's question and turns to Morris, "We can handle things from here. Thanks."

Morris pushes past Eric, his unit follows him and does the same, each one knocking him a little further back as they exit the apartment.

Zeke rushes into the room with a shoe box under his arm; he sees Eric, and his face takes a bad turn.

"What the hell are you doing here?" Zeke asks.

Eric concentrates on the box Zeke's holding. "Did you find something back there?"

"Why are you here? Do you have a warrant?" Zeke asks him.

Stone says, "I don't see a warrant, that means you two got to go."

Cannon's been growing more and more frustrated the entire time they were there. He storms out of the apartment; Eric doesn't know what to do, so he follows Cannon.

Shelly picks up something between Zeke and Eric. She asks, "What's up with you and Eric?"

The anger on Zeke's face hasn't changed, he tells her, "He claimed my parolee was involved in a drug transaction."

"What happened to him?" Stone asks.

Zeke shakes his head thinking about it, "The violation, made it easy for him to go back to jail."

"Why are you taking that case so hard?" Stone wonders.

Zeke tells him, "The parolee wasn't even in the city on that day."

"Eric lied …" Shelly says, "Now why doesn't that surprise me?"

"Yeah, and two days later, after lock up, he's knifed to death in his cell," Zeke adds.

Stone looks at Zeke. "What did the Department do with Eric's testimony?"

"The Department accepted his story, with him being a credible witness," Zeke states.

"Eric claimed to see the drug deal go down?" Stone questions Zeke.

Zeke throws his arm up, "The man had turned his life around and was expecting his first kid."

Shelly rubs Zeke's arm. "Sorry things went that way," she consoles him.

Stone asks to see the shoebox under Zeke's arm, asking him, "What's in there?"

Zeke takes it out and lifts off the lid saying, "It was under the bed."

He opens it, and it's filled with twenty-dollar bills neatly stacked to the brim.

Stone eyes the package and asks him, "How much is in there?"

"I stopped counting at eleven thousand," Zeke says.

Stone grows concerned, as he does the math dealing with the situation. "Oh boy, Tricky's in trouble, and he's on the run."

Shelly stares at the neatly stacked bills and scratches her head saying, "What has he gotten himself into now?"

"I think Cannon and his partner know something, something we don't know," Stone tells them.

"What do I do with all this cash?" Zeke asks.

"Hold on to it," Stone tells him.

"Hold on to it, where?" Zeke asks.

"Take it to your place …" Stone suggests.

"My place, are you crazy!" Zeke scoffs at the idea.

Shelly listens to them and questions Stone, "Seriously, why do you want Zeke to hold on to all this money?"

"Yeah?" Zeke asks, "Why not put in property?"

"We can't trust anyone outside of us," Stone tells them both.

"What are we going to do with it?" asks Shelly.

"Use it as bait …" Stone replies.

"Okay, in that case, I'll hold on to it," Shelly tells them.

"That's a good idea, Shelly. No one would suspect you of having Tricky's stash," Stone tells her.

Stone kneels, takes out his knife and cuts out an area of the rug he was inspecting earlier, sniffs it and places it in a separate evidence bag and gives it to Zeke along with the evidence bag holding the bloody revolver.

"Why cut up the rug?" Shelly asks, "I don't think Tricky will appreciate that, should he ever come back."

"With the money in that shoebox; he won't have trouble buying another rug. Anyway, there's something about this area," he tells Shelly, pointing out the difference between other parts of the rug.

"Looks like a rushed cleaning job," Shelly says.

"This shell casing and the blood-stained gun has a story to tell," Stone explains.

"Where did you find the gun?" Zeke asks.

"Over there peeking its barrel out just beneath the curtain in the corner by the window in the other room. Take these to Rico and tell him I need a rush job." Stone says, passing the evidence bags to Zeke.

An hour later, Zeke shows up in forensics and walks over to Ricardo "Rico" Perez, mid-thirties, handsome, single and for some women hard to resist. Stone feels he's the best chemist in forensics, known for his thorough work habits.

Rico spends his time working his magic, pouring different chemical solutions over the gun, the shell casing and the piece of carpet. He is getting fingerprints, blood compositions and a story of what might've had occurred at the scene of the crime.

His microscopic inspection of the blood samples and whatever was on the rug sample gave him a vivid idea of the number of people involved. After a visit to the crime scene and his return to the lab, he decides to give Stone a call.

Stone is sitting at his desk when the phone rings. It's Rico starting the conversation with the rug sample when Stone adds, "I thought I smelled bleach?"

"You were correct," Rico informs him, "Someone tried to clean the place with various cleaners?"

Rico refers to his report, "I wasn't able to process the sample at first. There were some complications. I had better luck with the weapon."

Stone asks him, "What did you find?"

"I found three different blood types and a set of fingerprints," Rico tells him.

"Anything we can use?"

"Yeah, first, the casing you gave me didn't come from the gun you found, second, there were three types of blood on the gun and in the rug sample," Rico tells him.

"There were three types of blood in those samples?"

"Yeah, I went to the crime scene," Rico acknowledges.

"I was hoping you'd do that. What did you find?" Stone asks.

"I see there was a guy there who used quite a bit of pure cocaine. How he didn't overdose, I don't understand?" Rico points out.

"What else did you come up with?"

"Well, it appears that one of the three individuals involved must be dead," Rico reads more information from his report.

"What makes you say that?" Stone inquires.

"One of them just lost too much blood, and whoever that somebody was, they were on medication," Rico continues reading from his report.

"You don't mean 'prescribed' medication?"

"Yeah, they were on Thorazine, it had to come from a doctor," Rico elaborated.

"Rico, you did a great job," Stone compliments him and asks, "Anyway of finding out who that might be?"

"A body would help, but I'll tell you what, I'll personally come over and hand you this report with the fingerprint information. Zeke told me to keep this on the 'low-low.' You do with it what you want," Rico tells Stone.

"Oh, one more thing," Rico quickly added.

"What's that?"

"The fingerprints on the weapon belong to a Cory Soriano."

"Really? I've heard of him." Stone tells him.

"Yeah? Well the thing is, there's a red flag on his file."

"What?"

"Yeah, a red flag. It seems the Feds need him, he's not to be arrested until the can accumulate enough evidence on him, that he'll be turncoat on his boss, Hugo 'Tiny' Barnett."

"Are you sure?"

"That's what I got, man. Just letting you know."

"Great job, thanks again, Rico," Stone tells him.

"You owe me, big time for this," Rico laughs.

"At the very least," Stone confirms.

Tricky's Tracks

Cannon is about to leave his office; he places some folders away on the rack on his desk and gets up. The phone rings as he is putting on his coat, he picks up the receiver.

"Detective Cannon, speaking," he answers.

"I heard you're looking for a guy?" a question is fed to him, it was Money.

"Who is this?" Cannon insists on knowing.

"A friend of the Boss," Money continues, disguising his voice.

"What do you want?" Cannon start showing interest.

"Concentrate on the girlfriend; she's at North General Hospital." The call ends with a click on the other connection. Eric comes into his office and sees a bothered look etched on Cannon's face.

"What's going on?" he asks Cannon.

Cannon takes his hat off the rack, turns Eric around and tells him, "We're off the North General, let's go."

It's growing dark outside as Tricky scurries into the hospital and works his way to the bank of elevators without catching the eye of security. After taking the elevator to the eleventh floor, he exits, peers over the rim of his shades, and sees the nursing station vacant. He goes over to the desk, looks over the log book to see that Rita is in room 1122. Tricky cautiously walks up the corridor checking the room numbers.

When he reaches the room, he sees his reflection in the glass door; his clothes are wrinkled and bloody. He does his best to wipe away the wrinkles out of his clothes. He stares at the room door and prepares himself for what might be awaiting him on the inside.

Tricky enters the room, looks beyond the open curtain and sees Rita sleeping. He walks over to her bed and does something he hadn't done in years; he starts to weep, unable to stop the steady flow of tears. He knew the situation would move him, he had prepared for it, but not this … he wasn't prepared for this.

Rita has several IVs in her arm and a tube up her nose.

Tricky lays his head down next to hers.

He begins shaking from the pain he's feeling and grabs her hand saying, "It's all my fault."

He succumbs to his feelings and pleads, "Please, please come out of this … I need you!"

Tricky doesn't notice Rita's eye twitching. He goes on sniffling, "We'll be together, I promise."

After a while, Rita starts to stir, and the image of Tricky gradually grows clearer. She notices his eyes are puffy, blood-shot red, and he has bruises on his cheeks.

Rita squeezes his hand and does her best to say something to him, "You're hurt."

Tricky looks at her with his tired, tear-stained

eyes. He weeps with joy at seeing her awake, but he tells her, "Hi baby, I'm fine."

Rita squeezes his hand tighter and urges him, "Baby, you've got to get out of here."

Tricky dismisses her advice and says, "Don't talk, you need your strength."

"But, they might've followed you!" she insists beginning to show fear in her eyes.

Confidently, Tricky tells her, "Don't worry, I can take care of myself."

Rita grows more anxious and insistent, "You gotta get out of here!"

Her anxiety causes her to start choking; the monitor starts signaling the nurses at the nursing station. A nurse quickly enters the room.

"Sir, visiting hours are over," the nurse informs Tricky.

Stilling choking, Rita pleads with him, "You've got to go ..."

A second nurse rushes into the room. She administers some medicine and adds something to Rita's IV bag.

Tricky reluctantly leaves, but as far as the second nurse is concerned, he's not moving fast enough.

"Sir, you have to leave now!" she orders.

The first nurse picks up the phone, "Security, to room 1122; Security to room 1122."

Tricky sees that Rita is out cold; he leaves the room and takes off.

A short while later, the elevator opens; Cannon and Evans exit and approach the nurse's station. The nurse on duty, the second nurse who had attended Rita earlier, is going over the log book, she looks up.

She informs them, "Visiting hours are over."

"Which room is Rita Coles in?" Cannon asks, flashing his badge.

"She unable to see anyone at this time," the nurse declares.

"What's the room number," Cannon says, refusing to take no for an answer.

The nurse assumes a defiant posture. "What did I just tell you."

Eric snatches the log book out of her hand, "Let us be the judge of that." He checks the log book for Rita's room number.

"Do you see her name there?" asks Cannon.

"She's in room 1122," Eric tells him.

Cannon and Evans walk up the corridor. The nurse waits until they leave, then grabs the phone and calls security.

Cannon and Evans enter the room; they look past the partly open curtain and see Rita in the same condition Tricky found her. She's unconscious. Evans goes over to her bed and leans over her.

There's a wicked and perverted smile on his face as he whispers over Rita's body, "I know you can hear me. Where is your boyfriend?"

Rita remains motionless.

Cannon looks at Evans and is a little disgusted

at his behavior; he tells him, "We're not going to get anything from her."

The door to Rita's room opens as four huge security officers march into the room followed by the two nurses. Eric goes for his weapon but stops short as Cannon flashes his badge.

The head security officer tells them, "You guys know better."

Cannon puts out his hands in a peaceful gesture, "Easy boys, we're on the same team."

The nurse wasn't having it, scolding them to the officers, "I told them, she couldn't see anyone, and they disrespected me!"

The security officer tells them, "You guys gotta go; it's as simple as that." He didn't look like he was a person to mess with, considering his size.

His partner adds, "Come on fellas, we got a job to do."

Cannon heads for the door with Evans following behind; then Cannon remembers to ask the nurse, "Did she have any visitors?"

"Yes, I had to chase him out too," she says.

Finally, some good news brings a smile to Cannon's face, he asks, "How long ago?"

Though the nurse is still annoyed with him, she answers, "About twenty minutes ago."

Eric is delighted, telling Cannon, "He still might be in the area."

He and Cannon race out of the room.

Decisions, Decisions

It's late afternoon, and the Mayor is holding a meeting with city officials and members of his staff; his Budget Committee and two deputies. Stacy, the clerk, passes out a folder to the attendees, then she resumes her role as a stenographer and prepares to take the minutes.

The Mayor has Wanda on his left and Dr. Leo Fairgood on his right. The other attendees are Adam Butler of The New York City Comptroller's Office; Jimmy Lewis, representing The City Council as their Chairman; Sidney Wells, a representative for the M.T.A.; and Martin Waters, Chairman of the Finance Committee, and the Mayor's personal accountant. All of them read through the proposal placed in front of them.

Leafing through the final pages, Wanda tells the Mayor, "I think it's a wonderful plan."

"Personally, I think this job should've been given to the City Council and me to look over," Jimmy Lewis flatly states.

Martin denounces that idea, "Jimmy, you're not an accountant."

"We have accountants on the Council," Jimmy corrects him.

The Mayor turns to his left, "Wanda, what's your assessment of this project?"

Jimmy cuts in, before Wanda can answer, questioning the Mayor, "Your Honor, is this a wise decision with the election a few months away?"

Adam offers his opinion, "Don't you think the Controller should be involved in a venture like this?"

"I thought that's why we for sent you," the Mayor answers him.

Finally, Wanda gets a chance to speak, "Your Honor, it takes great strides to get the substance abuser off drugs and go into a rehabilitation program."

Adam is going over some of the figures shown in the expense details and asks, "Your Honor, how would the City finance this endeavor?"

"Let me worry about that. Tell your boss; I expect his support on this," the Mayor clarifies to Adam.

Dr. Fairgood finally speaks, telling Adam, "The Controller's Office will need to work with Martin on the finalization of our plans."

Martin questions him, "That's why I'm here?"

Fairgood nods to him, letting him know the reason behind Martin's presence.

The Mayor pushes back his chair and tells Wanda, "Send the proposal to all City Officials.

Stacy, the stenographer, checks her watch and reminds the Mayor, "Your Honor, you have another meeting in a half hour."

The Mayor rises to his feet, nods to everyone. "So, if there's no other business to address, we can close this one out. Thank you all for attending, I'll keep you informed."

The Mayor starts to rub his hands together (his way of wrapping things up), Stacy grabs her equipment and tells the rest of them, "Lady and gentlemen, this meeting is over."

The committee files out of the room.

"Oh Wanda, before you go. You got a few minutes?" the Mayor asks her.

She remains seated.

Then to Leo, he says, "Let me know if you need anything."

Leo lingers for a moment then says, "Oh, yes. Thanks, your Honor. Good evening, Wanda."

The Mayor watches Dr. Fairgood walk away, waiting for him to get out of earshot, then turns to Wanda with a questionable expression on his face. "Are you sure about this thing?" he asks her.

She looks at him, gets up and begins to put her papers in order and tells him, "Honestly, your Honor, I don't know if the project will work, but I do know Leo has put in quite a bit of work and this is a very good idea."

The Mayor began to feel a lot better, "That's all I needed to know, thanks. Now go home and get some rest."

Adam's Apple

Tiny sits in his lavishly furnished room; he stands up wearing his tailor-fitted bathrobe, toweling his head while holding a phone to his ear. He nods now and then and offers a few "uh huh's." He strolls over to his penthouse window and looks out on the city he loves and on the neighborhood he owns. After the conversation is over, he disappointedly lets the phone drop to his side.

He takes a final look at the city skyline and storms back to his couch and dials Adam Butler's number.

Adam is seated at his desk in his home office going over some last-minute, paperwork. His phone rings, Adam stares at it, but for some unknown reason, he's uncomfortable about the call. He grabs his drink to his left and finishes it before picking up the receiver.

"Hello, Butler residents," he says.

"Why are you so hard to reach?" It's Tiny, his voice is mild, but holding back a rage that Adam would prefer not to hear.

"How did you get this number?" Adam asks him, trying not to sound offensive.

"Never mind that. When were you planning on telling me, we lost the shelter?"

Adam gulps and nervously pours himself another drink, "I, I couldn't do anything about that. The Mayor wants that property. You realize it does belong to the City?"

"You assured me that place was mine!" Tiny storms.

"When it comes to what the Mayor wants, what could I do?" Adam points out.

"So, it\s fuck me and give him what he wants." Tiny pauses long enough to drive home his point. Then he tells Adam, "You're going to have to do something about this."

Click! The line goes dead.

Tiny stares out on the city, he decided to wait on Adam's next move before calling his man Cory.

Adam puts down his phone, grows concerned, gets up and walks around his room, cursing under his breath. How did he ever get himself under Tiny's thumb? He knew the answer all too well, his greed and personal lust for women was just enough for Tiny to set the bait and lead him right into the trap he was standing in.

If there was only some way, he could turn the tables on Tiny. He looks out onto the City lost in a search for an advantage; any advantage.

Baby Girl

At Stone's house, the television is watching itself, while Stone is trying his best to carry a tune in his shower, something he's learned he should only do when he's alone. He turns the shower off, and fortunately for anyone within earshot he stops his singing, as he steps out of the shower with a towel wrapped around his waist, his phone rings. He rushes over to it and grabs the receiver.

"Hello, Stone's residence," he answers.

"Hi, Daddy," laughs Samantha, his daughter. She's a young, pretty preteen, who strongly resembles her mother; an "A" student and known as Sam by her friends. She has a jovial nature and is always excited when talking to her father, who she loves immensely.

"How's my favorite girl?" Stone laughs back.

"I'm doing good," she says, then quickly bragging to her father, "I got three A's for this marking period."

"Wow, I'm so proud of you!" Stone tells her, knowing how she loves to him hear him say those words and because he is.

"Daddy, you'll have Franklin and me all to yourself for the Christmas holidays, Mommy wants us to go over to Harold's house for Thanksgiving," Samantha informs him.

"And just how do you know that?" he asks.

"Mommy and her friend are going away for Christmas," she answers him. There's a hint of anger in her voice.

On the other end of the line, Stone quietly grits his teeth thinking about his wife with that numbskull, but he doesn't want his daughter to know how he feels about, so he fakes it, saying, "Oh really. Where is your mother?"

"She went to Franklin's school; it's Parent's Night."

"How's Franklin doing?" Stone asks her.

"Oh Daddy, you know I make sure he has good grades, he's my little brother," she assures him.

"That's great honey; I love the way you look out for him. Tell Franklin; I'm proud of him too. I'll see you guys tomorrow,"

"What about Mommy?" Samantha asks him.

"Tell your mother, I'll call her."

"Good night, Daddy, love you," Samantha says.

"Good night love you too," Stone says blowing her a kiss.

After the call, Stone gets up and goes back into the bathroom to finish up. He stops by the mirror and looks at himself, replays in his head the conversation with his daughter and tells the mirror image of himself, "You fucked up, yeah you! Losing your connection to your children and having to live a life with this bullshit arrangement, only to pretend its normal? You fucked up! Ahh!"

He throws the towel at the mirror and walks out of the bathroom to pour himself a drink.

Overnight Delivery

John Stone sits behind his desk finishing up a cup of coffee. It's early morning, and he's getting his files ready for cataloging when Zeke rushes into his office, overly excited and plops himself down on the seat across from him.

Stone looks at his boyish grin and asks, "What are you so happy about?"

Zeke smacks his hands together and jumps up, "Out Mister Brown is downstairs."

Stone jumps up and quickly follows Zeke downstairs. When they reach the first floor, Stone doesn't see anyone closely resembling Tricky. "Where? I don't see shit, where is he?"

"Follow me," Zeke grabs Stone by the arm and leads him out the front door. There, off to the side of the building entrance, in a worn, partly flattened cardboard box was Tricky, in a drug-induced sleep.

Many of the incoming parolees avoid Tricky's slumber wagon; they walk into the building paying no attention to the man in the box, a familiar sight for too many of them. Stone calls two officers out to Tricky's spot, they pick him up, he's barely awake, and they carry him inside.

When they get him to his feet, Tricky wakes just

long enough to give Stone a weak wave and smile, while uttering, "Officer Stone, I'm here."

An hour and several cups of strong coffee later, Tricky's in a holding room; he's slumped over a table. The two officers, who helped carry him inside, stand near the door. Stone leans against a wall, carefully watching Mister Brown. Tricky has a hard time keeping his eyes open.

When Tricky starts to stir, Stone takes a seat in front of him and asks, "What happened at your apartment?"

Tricky mumbles, "I couldn't let him shoot me too. I waited for the chance to shove a nail file right into his eye."

"Who? Who is he?" Stone demands to know.

"They'll be coming after me ..." Tricky squeals, before losing consciousness.

One of the officers asks Stone, "Who is he talking about?"

The other officer concludes, "It's the drugs talking."

"Take him to a holding cell," Stone tells them. Stone had an idea from what Rico told him, but he didn't want to divulge any information to these guys.

The two officers take Tricky out of the room and down the hall.

Tricky looks like he just came out of a trash bin. His clothes were dirty, worn and ragged, with every type of stain imaginable along with obvious blood stains. Stone can see Tricky deserves better than this; he feels sorry for him, seeing him in this state.

Stone finds himself back in his office going over Carlton Brown's folder. All of a sudden, he grabs the phone.

"Hello, Prevention. How may I help you?" the secretary says answering Stone's call.

"Director Richards, please," he tells her.

"Who may I say is calling?"

"Parole Officer Stone."

"Thank you; please hold."

Stone is hoping to reach Milton Richards, someone well versed in the use of illegal substances. He's in his 50's and a former addict, alcoholic, and crackhead who's been clean for more than eleven years. If anyone stayed in a conversation for too long with Milton, he was bound to mention that fact somewhere along the way. Milton Richards has been the Director of the Prevention Program for over twenty years.

Milton's currently in a supervisor's meeting with a Substance Abuse Counselor. Sam Coles, a former crackhead who has been clean for seven years; stares as Milton goes over his report.

Milton finishes the report and looks up at Coles, "Sam, this is good."

"Thank you, sir," Coles tells him.

The intercom beeps on the office phone.

Richards tells Sam to excuse him as he takes the call.

"Parole Officer Stone is on line one," the secretary tells him.

Richard turns to Sam, "Supervision's over. Good job."

"Thank you, sir," Coles tells Richards as he gathers his papers and leaves the office.

Richards continues his conversation with Stone, "Stone, good to hear from you. How's it going?"

Stone doesn't answer the question, but reflects with, "Milton, how are things with you?"

"Ah, things could be better," Richards tells him.

"What's wrong?" Stone inquires.

"I have to let go two of my best workers," he confesses.

"Why fire them, if they're your best?"

"Budget cuts …"

"Sorry to hear that. You and your people do good work," Stone compliments him.

"Enough about my problems. How can I help you?" asks Richards.

"Are you still accepting referrals?" questions Stone.

"As long as I'm here," Richards chuckles.

"I need to give a guy a second chance," Stone tells him.

"You're still trying to save lives …"

"Look who's talking …"

Richards chuckles again, "What's this guy's name?"

"Carlton Brown."

"When can you get him here?"

"Today," Stone tells him.

"Send him over. I'll be here, waiting,"

Stone is grateful. "Thanks, Milton."

"What are friends for …"

Unexpected Lesson

Hours later, Stone is sitting at his desk going over some files, when his door's opens, and Marcus Thurman walks in, looking like he's got an ax to grind. He's dressed to the nines and is somewhat taller than Stone. He's an imposing figure and uses his size to intimidate and bully others around him. "Throw men" is an appropriate nickname for him. He's also Stone's boss. Thurman comes and stands over him.

"I know what you did with Carlton Brown. You're going to take him out of that program and put his ass in jail," he orders Stone.

"He needs treatment for his addiction," Stone tells him.

"He's a criminal. Fuck his addiction!" Thurman barks.

Stone looks straight, yet defiantly at him and says, "I'm not going to change my decision."

Thurman curses; he steps back and takes off his jacket. Stone gets out of his chair. Thurman shoves his finger less than an inch from Stone's face.

"You need me to teach you a lesson ..." Thurman says, swinging his arm at Stone.

Stone easily evades Thurman's punch and grabs his arm and flips Thurman over the desk. He holds

Thurman's arm to keep him from falling to the floor. There's a knock on the door; Stone releases Thurman, who falls on his ass. Zeke enters with Officer Newton. They look and realize that an altercation must've taken place, but they behave as though nothing happened.

Newton goes to Thurman and says, "Sir, let me help you. You must've fallen."

Newton helps Thurman to his feet. Stone's phone rings and Zeke scurries over to pick up the receiver. Thurman angrily yanks his jacket and puts it on.

"Officer Stone's office. Yes, sir. I'm fine …, sure he's right here." Zeke turns to Stone offering him the receiver; he tells him, "It's the Mayor's Office."

He hands the phone to Stone, who takes it, but doesn't take his eyes off Thurman. Thurman stares back at Stone in a threatening manner, giving him a "this ain't over" look.

He excuses himself by saying, "I'm late for another appointment …" Thurman dismisses Newton's assistance and barks, "Get out of my way!" He storms out of the office.

Stone is cooling down but is still breathing hard from an adrenalin rush, "Hello, Stone here," he answers.

It's Dr. Fairgood on the other end. "Stone, what's going on there? You sound winded."

"I was just moving some junk around," Stone tells him.

"James, we need to meet," Leo tells him.

Leo, I can't, not according to this schedule. I don't have the time," admits Stone.

Zeke, who is listening to some of the conversation, whispers to him, "You're talking to the Deputy Mayor …"

Stone gives Zeke a shrug and moves to sit at his desk, hoping to give himself a little more private space. He tells Leo, "I won't be free for another week."

"Leo, however, doesn't want to hear any excuses, he's serious, "James, let's cut to the chase, your career's on the line."

"I don't understand …" Stone blurts out, somewhat confused.

"Zita's tomorrow at noon. Don't be late!" Fairgood tells him and ends the call.

Shelly and Stone finally get a chance to have dinner together and the night is young, but it's not what Shelly expected. It wasn't the usual spirited conversation that she enjoyed when they shared each other's company. Stone, for the most part, had very few words to say as he appeared lost in thought.

A waiter comes and clears the table, serving them coffee. Shelly watches Stone stare off into space. She feels she has to say something,

"What's going on? You've been strangely quiet all evening?"

Stone puts his coffee down. "Thurman showed up today," he sighs.

"I heard," Shelly adds.

"I showed him an unexpected lesson," Stone says, giving her a wink and a faint smile.

Shelly's surprised to hear it, "You two were fighting?"

Stone nonchalantly shrugs his shoulders. "The man fell over my desk."

"Well, if you say that's what happened, fine," she chuckles. Shelly leans back shaking her head after a few sips of her coffee.

Stone's mood gets a little darker when he says, "Doctor Fairgood called."

"The Deputy Mayor?" she asks.

Stone gives her a nod. "He insists, we meet for lunch tomorrow."

She puts her coffee down, leans forward on the table and ponders for a moment. "You two know each other, right?"

"Yeah, we grew up in the same neighborhood," Stone tells her.

"What do you think he wants?"

Stone appears to hesitate, as if he would prefer not to tell her, so he says, "I'm not quite sure …"

Shelly presses further, "Well, then what did he say?"

Stone finishes his coffee, looks at Shelly and says what he thinks, "It's not what he said, it was the way he said it, — my career's over."

"What? What does he mean by that?" Shelly responds, worried.

"The word is out, Thurman's working to get me fired," Stone confesses. He sits back and remains quiet; he stares off again.

Shelly avoids making eye contact; she stares at the empty glass of water. She wanted to know what was on Stone mind; now she does, and now, it's on her mind. They both sit there in a quiet, thoughtful mood.

Final Notice

Stone walks through the double doors of the New York State, Department of Parole building. He sees a few parolees are waiting to see their parole officers. Stone walks up to the security desk. Newton smiles at him.

"Good morning, Officer Stone," Newton greets him.

"Good morning, Newton," Stone returns the greeting.

Stone continues walking down the corridor to his office. He enters his office and finds an envelope on his desk.

He tears it open and reads:

To: Parole Officer John Stone
From: Marcus Thurman, Director of The New York State Department of Parole

Enclosed is a list of men on your caseload. These men violated their parole.

It is your duty to arrest these men and have them incarcerated for their violation. I'm available to address this matter with you, on how they are to be taken into custody for incarceration. You have six days to fulfill this mandate.

Failure to comply or if your performance is deemed unsatisfactory, will lead to your termination from this department.

Stone lets loose a few well-chosen curse words and tosses the paper into the wastebasket. He's riled up and paces the room looking for something to hurt — his phone rings. He stares at it and waits; it rings again. He quickly moves to get the receiver before it rings a third time.

"Good morning, Stone speaking."

"Don't miss our meeting." It's Dr. Fairgood.

"I'll see you there," Stone tells him.

Leo hangs up.

Stone leaves the office early; he's in a long-walking mood. It's noon by the time he gets to Zita's Café, there's a line of people waiting to get in and the place is packed. Leo's sitting at a table and glances at his watch; it's 12:07 pm. A familiar waitress is at his table.

"Good afternoon, Doctor Fairgood, would you like a drink, while you're waiting?" she asks him.

"Eh, yes, thank you," he responds.

"Gin, grenadine, and lemon on the rocks?" she queries to make sure, though she is already acquainted with his drink,

Leo smiles and nods; the waitress hurries off. Stone enters, sees Leo and works his way through the crowd to sit across from Leo, without saying a word. He nods, and Leo returns a nod.

"There's a paper trail on you," Leo informs him.

"Does it matter?" Stone says; he could care less.

"Thurman can make things difficult for you. However, I got a job for you," Leo tells Stone.

"Doing what?"

"The Haven Shelter needs a new ..."

"The one in Brooklyn?" Stone interrupts.

"You've heard of the place?"

"Yeah, it's a real hell hole," Stone comments, already sounding disappointed with the offer.

Dr. Fairgood goes on, "The place needs a new Director."

"To do what?"

"Make it a real, viable program."

"What if I don't work out?" Stone asks Fairgood.

"Our careers, yours and mine, depend on you making it a real program. What do you say?" Leo confides in him.

"Is that the only thing on the menu?" Stone asks.

"That and what they're serving here," Leo tells him, offering him his hand and a smile.

Stone's serious look fades to offer Leo a smile; he takes Leo's hand and says, "Let's look at the menu and order something."

They both laugh and call the waitress over to take their orders.

Next Steps

A few days have gone by; Stone's office is bare, just a few boxes remain, stacked by the door. Zeke enters; sees Stone cleaning out his desk.

Stone looks up and tells him, "Say goodbye to this place."

"Are we sure about this move?" Zeke asks him, showing concern.

"If there's one thing, I seem to be learning the hard way; it's you can't be sure about anything," Stone offers Zeke.

"Amen to that," Zeke comments.

Zeke grabs a few boxes and heads out. Stone gets the rest and takes one final look at the place; then turns out the lights.

When he gets to the elevator that Zeke is holding for him, Zeke poses a question, "I'm surprised, Thurman isn't here to see you off?"

"Why?" Stone asks, "He's getting what he wanted, my ass out the door."

"Yeah, but not to be here gloating, just doesn't seem like Thurman," Zeke commented.

"Yeah, now that you mentioned it, it doesn't," Stone added. "Anyway, thanks for the help Zeke, I need to say goodbye to a few folks in the building, I'll call you later."

"Sure, no problem, any time. We'll talk," Zeke tells him and waves as he leaves.

Its night and Stone is sitting on his sofa, watching television. The program is interrupted by a special news bulletin!

"Sanitation Worker Finds the Body of a Man in Garbage!"

The announcer on the TV screen reports, "Today a man's body was found rolled in a rug near the Brooklyn docks."

A photograph of the slain man, Lloyd Harvey, comes on the screen, and the announcer continues with his report, "Mr. Lloyd Harvey was employed at the Haven Treatment Shelter."

The news camera displays a body going into an ambulance surrounded by pedestrians and uniformed police. The announcer goes on, "There's no apparent reason for Mister Harvey's death. According to the Police, they currently have no suspects or leads in the case. We'll return after this station break."

Stone changes the station a few times, only to discover the report is on those channels as well. He grabs the phone and calls Zeke.

Zeke's home reading "The Twelve Steps," to get a better handle on trying to understand the nuances of addiction, when the phone rings.

"Hey, Zeke, it's Stone."

"Hey, what's up?" Zeke responds.

"If you got a quick sec, turn your television to Channel 5 News," Stone tells him.

"Why? What's up?" Zeke questions.

"Just turn, will you," Stone insists.

"Okay, I got it on. I see that a guy who was at the Haven Treatment Shelter, got killed. Damn, that's our place. What's on your mind?" Zeke says, surprised, but also aware that Stone has something up his sleeve.

"I'll pick you up in a half hour," Stone says.

Stone and Zeke arrive at the Haven Treatment Shelter sometime later that evening. They keep a discrete distance from where they can remain unnoticed and still watch the activities. From Stone's van, they see drug dealers, hustlers, and gangsters push their way into the facility. All the people are dressed for the evening as they disappear behind closed doors.

Stone passes Zeke his pair of binoculars so that Zeke can get a better look.

"Damn, who knows about this?" Zeke asks.

"I can tell one thing for sure," Stone whispers.

"What's that," questions Zeke.

"Somebody has to know something," Stone replies.

"Yeah, and I know something else. We're gonna need a kick-ass team for this job," Zeke tells Stone, giving him back the binoculars.

"Leave that up to me." Stone gives Zeke a confident nod.

Giving Thanks

Thanksgiving had arrived sooner than expected, and the Stone family is gathering at the home of Stone's sister and her husband, Candice and Adam Butler. Some of the family felt that having the Thanksgiving feast at Glenn Stone's home would bring back to many heartfelt memories of their youngest son Ricky who recently passed away, and show-boating Adam jumped at the opportunity to be in control of the situation. Everyone was dealing with the pain of Kirks loss in their own way. Many felt a change of scenery would offer some healing.

The women and some of the younger relatives were setting up the table which held a huge, baked turkey, surrounded by steaming potatoes, brown sugar pineapples over ham, tender, baked yams and an assortment of other delicious dishes.

John Stone assists his father, Frank, to the head of the table, maneuvering Frank's wheelchair passed the household furniture to lift him up and onto the seat.

Frank thanks him and then asks, "John, I noticed that your wife and the kids aren't with us today. Where are they?"

"Eh, the wife? Oh, she and the kids went to spend Thanksgiving with her family upstate." Stone never really liked the idea of lying to his dad, but he was caught off-guard, and it was the best thing he could come up with in such short notice.

"Well tell them, grandpa says hi," Franks tells him.

"Will do dad, will do," John answers.

After getting his father seated at the head of the table, Stone goes to help in the kitchen, pitching in by taking out two hot pans of biscuits from the oven and taking them to the table. Some of the family women give him a nod of thanks.

Glenn comes in from the living room; he's disappointed that his favorite football team is two touchdowns behind in the game. He plops himself down in the seat on his father's right, huffing and mumbling obscenities under his breath. He holds the seat next to him for his wife, Susan.

"What wrong, Glenn?" his father asks him.

"Team ain't worth shit, no defense and then they throw an interception." Glenn shakes his head.

Glenn happens to look up and sees his wife bringing more things to the table. Susan, a good woman in her early forties, has been married to Glenn for more than sixteen years.

As Susan works her way around the table, she places a dish of cranberry sauce near Adam, who waves her off, saying, "Hey, take that away from me, I hate that shit!"

Glenn, who always hated his brother-in-law and was against the idea of having Thanksgiving dinner at his house, looks up at Adam and stares. Adam catches his glare. Glenn quietly growls, "Watch how you talk to my wife!"

Adam does his best to avoid Glenn's cold stare; he decides to get up and pour himself a drink, spending enough time at the bar to let things cool down and allow himself time to ease back to the table.

Meanwhile Frank is trying to handle one of the hot biscuit pans and jerks his hand back in pain. John leans over with a mitten on, "Let me help you with that, Pop."

Glenn watches John pandering to his father's needs and gets annoyed with him.

"Let the women do that," Glenn tells his brother.

"Yeah, you're making us look bad," jokes Adam.

Glenn motions to Adam with a nod, "You do that all by yourself."

The women finish up and sit next to their husbands, calling everyone else to the table.

Stone takes a seat on the other side of his father.

Candice looks around to make sure everyone is seated; she stands and offers grace, "Heavenly Father, we give thanks for bringing us here together to celebrate this family holiday. This has been a year of hardship, a year of loss. We know that you have accepted the spirit of our brother Kirk. Please let him know that he's missed and that his family loves him very much and always will. We ask that you watch over the members of our family who could not be here with us today.

"We ask that this food is blessed and that we have

a bountiful year that offers answers and reunites us in love and strength. Amen."

Everyone follows with, "Amen."

Adam congratulates her, saying, "Honey, that was a wonderful prayer."

Glenn usually takes it upon himself to assume the role of "cutter of the turkey," since Thanksgiving, is typically held at his house. Out of habit, Glenn reaches for the carving knife, but Adams cuts him off with, "What are you doing?"

"I'm going to cut the turkey," Glenn tells him.

"I," Adam defiantly reminds him, "I do the carving in this house!" He gives Glenn a look, letting him know who's the king of the castle around here.

Glenn gets up and storms out of the room in a huff. Susan excuses herself and runs after him. There's a hush around the table.

Adam doesn't apologize for his behavior; he expects everyone to understand. "What?" he says, looking around the room, "My house, my turkey!"

Candice attempts to appeal to his better nature, "Oh, Honey, you didn't have to say that."

Adam gives her a defiant look, "Your brother's not running my house, period!"

Stone quietly mumbles underneath his breath, "So much for reuniting the family in love and strength."

After a minute or two, Susan coaxes Glenn back to the table, and Adam begins carving the turkey. Adam knows he hit Glenn where it hurts, and he carves slow enough, knowing Glenn is watching. He's enjoying it as family members pass the plates. Other family members mumble at the goings-on.

Things calm down, and Adam is feeling cocky, now that he's back to being the head honcho. It's all about power and control, even at holiday affairs.

He calls across the table to Stone, "I hear you're working for the Mayor."

Stone has been aware of this power-play since he got there; he sees where it's going, and he doesn't want to play into it. He tells Adam, "I'm working 'with' the Deputy Mayor."

"That's my brother …" Candice says, hoping to squash the conversation.

"Johnny has always gone beyond our expectations," Susan adds, not catching Candice's queue.

Glenn, who's been sitting with a bad mood for the last few minutes, comes out of left field and asks John, "So, Johnny, are you and your wife back together?"

Stone gives him a cold stare and there is a surprising hush that fills the room as though a tiger broke free from its cage.

Frank breaks the silence by asking Stone, "Johnny, you and Victoria are separated?"

Candice angrily leans in Glenn's direction, "You said, you'd never mention that!"

"I never told you that," Glenn says defensively.

"Why did you bring that up now?" Susan asks him. Her husband's behavior throws her.

"You're seeing your children, right?" his father, Frank, asks.

Glenn looks at his father mocking him, "You're one to talk, are you seeing all of your children?"

"Of course, he is, we're all here," Susan says attempting to defend Frank.

Susan is speechless and startled at what everyone is saying.

"We all knew," Candice confesses.

Adam looks at Candice and asks her, "Why didn't you tell me?"

"What difference would it have made," Candice interrupts.

"I'm your husband, I should've known," Adam answers her.

Frank turns to Stone, "So who's carving the turkey for my grandchildren, today?

"What?" Stone finds himself drowning in this nonsense; as it's all about a topic he never had any intention of discussing.

Glenn doesn't help by saying to Frank, "You weren't always with us on the holidays. At least they're separated."

Stone finds the direction and the tone of the conversation sickening; he excuses himself, gets up and leaves the house. He stands out on the porch and takes in the cool evening air. "What the fuck was that all about," he mutters to himself, "Damn!"

He stares up at the sky, realizing he could use a drink when Glenn comes out on the porch a few minutes behind him. Stone turns around to see who it is, upon seeing Glenn he tells him, "Say what's on your mind, you seem to have something that's got you by the ass."

"That fuckin' brother-in-law, Adam, can't stand his ass," Glenn tells him.

"So, you thought you'd fight back by putting my dirty laundry on the table?" Stone says looking at Glenn, pissed.

"Sorry, I was feeling shitty, so I acted shittily, but tell me, first you were a cop, then you were a Parole Officer. What's next?" Glenn voices his opinion.

"Since when are you so concerned about my job decisions?"

"You joined the force; Kirk joined the force. Why"

"I wanted to follow the family tradition, I thought Kirk wanted that as well," Stone tells Glenn.

"Kirk wanted to be like you, a free spirit. He didn't want to be a cop," Glenn says, standing next to Stone, looking out on the evening sky.

"He died trying to be a good cop," Stone says.

"Dad was always out doing his thing. He could've done something," Glenn tells him.

"Dad? What does Dad have to do with this?"

"He was out fathering another child," Glenn breaks the news to Stone.

"Where did you hear that?" Stone confronts him.

"Kirk told me we have another sister," Glenn tells him.

Stone pauses the conversation for a few seconds. "Really?" Stone's question wasn't one of surprise. It was more like a "What else is new?" kind of question.

"Who else knows about this?" Stone inquires of Glenn.

"I don't know."

"How did Kirk find out about her?"

"Supposedly, he was en route to meet up with an informant, a few years ago at a restaurant downtown and happened to see Dad talking to a young woman in military uniform. Kirk asked his informant if he could quietly work his way across the street to where they were, and he got close enough to pick up on their conversation." Glenn adjusts his stance and looks around to make sure no one is listening.

"And?" Stone says, egging him on.

"Well he did, and when he came back; he told Kirk that they were debating over family and she got angry and said, 'You're not my father, you never loved me!' And then he told her, 'I do love you, you don't understand my situation.'"

"Wow, that must've been rough on Kirk," Stone comments.

"I'm sure it was," Glenn sighs.

"Now that you know, what are you going to do about it?" Stone asks him.

"Let Dad keep his secret, I suppose," Glenn says, shrugging his shoulders.

"Have you even talked to him about it?" Stone puts him on point.

"No."

"Sorry Glenn, I'm not you; never were. I'm going to talk to Dad about it."

Glenn catches John by the arm; now Glenn somewhat regrets he told his brother the story. He tells him, "No, let him have his secret, just like everyone else."

"What's that supposed to mean?" Stone goes on the defensive.

"Isn't it a secret that you're taking a job with some damn drug addicts?" Glenn questions him.

"It's not a secret, just because I haven't mentioned it. I'm taking over a drug program." Stone tells him.

"Drugs. That's what got Kirk killed. He tried to stop them from selling that shit!" Glenn's eyes begin to tear.

Stone confesses to him, "Glenn, I could use your help, seriously … I think I can make a difference."

"What can I do?" he asks. He laments, "I wish Kirk could've used my help." To Stone, Glenn appears lost in thought.

"I need your help," Stone says to Glenn, only to see him shaking as he did at the funeral; Glenn begins to weep uncontrollably.

"Glenn, it's not your fault," Stone assures him.

"I couldn't help Kirk; I should've been there for him."

Stone embraces his brother in an attempt to comfort him, telling him, "Like always, Kirk wanted to work the case alone."

Glenn pulls away from him and talks through his tears, "I told him that assignment was too dangerous."

"He wanted to work undercover alone."

"He shouldn't have been alone ... He told me, I worried too much," Glenn adds.

"Well, I won't argue with him there," Stone chuckles, "but you've got to stop blaming yourself."

Stone gives Glenn an extra hug, pats him on the back and says, "Stay here, I'll be right back, going to talk to Dad." He heads back into the house.

Stone comes in and sees that Frank is finishing with his meal. "Dad, can we talk privately?"

"Eh, sure son, what's up? Anyway, I've eaten and I'm full to the brim, damn if I don't bust," Frank jokes.

"Here, Dad, let me help you back into your wheelchair." Stone helps his father toward the den. Adam watches them from his seat at the table, but he's too involved in a conversation with other relatives to interrupt them.

Once Stone gets him in the den, Frank asks, "So, what's up?"

Stone is very straightforward and direct with his father.

"When are you planning to tell us Dad, or were we supposed to find out at your funeral, that you have another daughter and we have another sister?"

Frank sits there in his wheelchair while his son eases into a seat across from him. Frank searches for the words he had been preparing to say whenever this day would come, and the subject brought up. He must have misplaced those words, because, for the life of him, he couldn't find them.

His thoughts raced back to that day years ago when he thought he saw Kirk walking across the avenue, while he had lunch with, Ada, his daughter. He always wondered if Kirk saw him; the thought always bothered him.

"Her name is Ada," it was all he could say, then he adds, "If you must know, I don't have any excuse. I knew this day would come eventually. I'm not proud I betrayed your mother's trust or her love, but I won't deny or apologize for my feelings for Ada's mother, Tracy. I'm not perfect, son, I never was. In some areas of life, I was successful, in others, I failed. I never gave any of my children the total love they deserved."

Frank's eyes tear up as he looks at Stone who also has tears in his eyes.

Stone clears his throat, "Thank you, Dad. I know it wasn't easy for you to say what you said, but I'm glad you did." Stone breathes a sigh of relief; the last thing he wanted to do was to hurt his father, but he's relieved it's out in the open.

Frank doesn't want to dwell on the subject any longer; he asks Stone, "So what were you and Glenn talking about on the porch if you don't mind me asking?"

"We were talking about the subject of a new sister and my new position as director of a drug program. I was asking Glenn for help, in fact, I need to go back out and finish our conversation," Stone says. He gives his father a brief rundown of who's presently occupying the Haven Shetler before getting out his seat.

As he approaches Frank to bring him back into the dining room, Frank takes his hand and tells him, "Ada, your sister can help you, trust me. I'll give her a call in the morning and let her know you'll be calling. Okay?"

"Okay, Dad."

Just as Stone opens the door to the den, Adam appears. Adam asks, "Can I help you two?"

"No, we finished, but thanks," Stone tells him while wheeling his father past him.

Stone comes back out on the porch, Glenn is seated and smoking on a cigar.

"How'd it go with Dad?" Glenn

"We came to an understanding, that's the most I can say for now," Stone tells him.

Stone reveals to Glenn the problem he may be facing in the takeover of the Haven Shelter.

"I know a cop that could help you."

"He won't be able to stay on the force," Stone makes it clear to Glenn.

"Not to worry; he won't be on the force much longer."

"What's his name?"

"Dan Harrison. Have you enlisted anyone yet." Glenn asks.

"I'm putting a team together," Stone tells him.

Family Matters

Frank decides to give his daughter a call that evening when he got home from Thanksgiving dinner. They hadn't spoken in years since there was a decline in Frank's health.

Ada Wade, an attractive, young woman in her late twenties is preparing to do some exercise on the floor of her large studio apartment. Her neatly arranged medals in martial arts, military awards and a medal of honor hang in an area of the room, while another area holds pictures of her mother and her at different times in their lives; from a young tomboy to a beautiful woman. She begins her routine when the phone rings; she rolls over backward and picks up the receiver.

"Yes?" she asks.

"How's my little girl?" asks Frank.

Ada's gets angry at hearing the sound of her father's voice, considering it's taken him so long to call her, but she respects him too much and the only response she can make is, "I'm not a little girl anymore."

"I know, you're grown up."

"You never came to see us. Why?" Her voice is tense but controlled.

"I sent gifts … money."

114

"That's not being there."

"I apologize, I did the best I could do," Frank explains.

"Did you ever tell your family about me?"

"You're not fair … but it seems some of them knew already. I spoke with John about you today," Frank confesses.

"Why did you call?

"John needs your help … or at least I told him you could help him. He needs you! With your military background; he stands a chance."

There's a moment spent with Ada recounting the empty years she longed to meet her half-brothers and half-sister.

"How did you know about the military?" she questions him.

"Remember we talked about it when you first enlisted."

"Oh yeah, seems so long ago." She recalls.

"Will you help him?"

"Tell him to call me …"

"Thanks, Honey! Tell your mother, hope she had a Happy Thanksgiving. Did you spend the day with her?"

"She died last summer," Ada says, breaking up. There's nothing else she could say to the man who once claimed he loved her mother. She glances at her mother's portrait on her mantle.

Frank hears the line go dead. Tracy died? Ada's statement courses through him as shame and loss merge in the pit of his stomach. He thought about what he told Johnny about his failures, here was another laid at his feet. He sits in his wheelchair and quietly weeps alone, more alone than he ever expected.

The Gathering

Morning finds Stone making phone calls to various contacts. He looks at his short list and sees the name of an old friend and his son's godfather, a Civil Service Investigator in his 40's. He makes the call.

"This could be really dangerous," he tells Andy.

"Come on, Stone; you didn't call me not to use me. What's the job and where do you want me?"

"Are you sure…?"

Andy stares at a group of pictures on his desk, one of them is Franklin, his godson. He gets up and goes to his gun cabinet.

"I could use a little something to do; things are getting boring around here. You know how a job can get sometimes. Count me in, whatever the job is," Andy tells Stone.

He removes an old fashioned .38 revolver from a holster and checks the chamber to see if it's loaded.

"Andy, thanks," says Stone.

"Call me when you're ready."

The day gets long with some maybes and some rejections, but for Stone, maybes aren't good enough; by evening he reaches Peter Duncan, a 62-year-old, former cop known as Duncan. He retired after thirty-six years on the force — there is a gun rack behind him as he sits in his den and picks up the phone with Stone on the other end.

"Peter, how are you? I got a job for you if you're interested," Stone says.

"Damn Stone, good hearing from you; I'm fine. When and where's the job?" Peter asks.

"It could be dangerous."

"You know me, I like dangerous," Peter chuckles.

The next day, Stone decides to pull out the number his father gave him; its time to call Ada, his sister. He talks a breath and prepares himself for the unknown.

Ada's going through some martial art routines when the phone rings; she grabs it.

"Hello," Ada says.

"Hello Ada, this is your brother, John," Stone tells.

"I've been expecting your call; Dad told me you needed some help," she tells him.

"This feels a little odd," Stone says, trying to judge Ada from the sound of her voice.

"It shouldn't. Let's face it; it's probably the only way we'll get the chance to meet each other. What do you need?" she sarcastically jokes to him.

Stone likes her attitude already; he fills her in on the operation.

Hearsay

It's called The Lounge; the place is dark and packed. People are on the dance floor; they move rhythmically to the funky music. Tyrone enters, pushing his way through the crowd. A few people turn away from him in disgust.

He gets to the bar and catches his reflection in the bar mirror; he's a mess. He pats his hair down, turns up his collar and begins looking for someone. He sees Speedy at the other end of the bar with a couple of ladies and works his way over to him.

He catches Speedy's attention and says, "I have important news for your boss."

"Tell me, and I'll tell him."

"There's no doubt in my mind that you'd convey my information, but that task is for me and me alone," Tyrone tells him.

Speedy is confused by Tyrone, saying, "What? Wait here."

"I'm not going anywhere."

Tyrone sees Speedy go in a side door. He catches another glimpse of himself in a mirror. He can't believe how he looks after he thought he'd patted his hair. It sprouted back up along with his collar. He sees Speedy returning.

"Come with me," Speedy tells him.

Tyrone follows Speedy through a side door. They enter a private lounge with a bar and music. Cory has his back to them; he's having a good time entertaining three "fine" young women. Cory turns to see them, and Tyrone notices the patch on his eye. While he stares at Cory's eyepatch, Cory is staring at his shameful attire.

"What are you doing here?" Cory demands an answer.

"I can charge you for what I know," Tyrone tells him.

"And why should I pay you anything?"

Tyrone clears his throat, saying, "My mouth is dry, I'm a little thirsty.

"You want a glass of water?"

"Nah, but I'd like a vodka and orange juice on the rocks," Tyrone lets out.

"Hey bartender," Cory calls and points to Tyrone, "Give him what he wants."

The bartender prepares Tyrone's drink.

"Thanks, you are a gentleman and …"

"Cut the bullshit. What do you have for me?" snaps Cory.

"There was a meeting this evening, and it might affect your business," Tyrone tells him after taking a sip of his drink.

"Is that all you got?"

"The Mayor's taking back the shelter."

"Are you sure about that?" Cory asks. He moves closer to Tyrone.

"I heard the Deputy Mayor announce the takeover."

"What do you want?" Cory asks Tyrone.

"Just some blow and another drink," Tyrone tells him.

Cory motions to Speedy, who leans into him, "Tell Willis, to give him a package and anything he wants to drink."

A grateful Tyrone offers a shallow bow and extends his hand, "Thank you …"

Cory looks at Tyrone's dirty fingers; he turns and walks away from him saying, "Speedy will show you out."

Cory rejoins his three lady friends, but his thoughts are on Tiny, as he wonders if Tiny know about this new update. He decides that he'll check it out for himself in the morning and see if Tyrone is on point with the info.

Tyrone and Speedy leave the private lounge and go out into the main area of the club. Tyrone walks up to the bar waving to catch the bartender's attention. Willis appears disgusted after seeing Tyrone. Speedy steps up to the bar.

"Willis, give him a package and a drink," Speedy tells Willis.

Willis looks at Speedy and asks, "What's up?"

"It's on Cory."

Willis gives Tyrone the once over; he frowns and mumbles what he's thinking, "Damn, they let anybody in here."

"What did you say?" asks Tyrone.

"What are you drinking? Willis says, ignoring the question.

"Give me a vodka and orange juice on the rocks and a C-note with the package."

Speedy catches sight of a lady friend and tells Tyrone, "I gotta go."

Willis keeps staring at Tyrone while preparing his drink. Meanwhile, Tyrone is admiring a woman seated a seat from him. When she turns her head in his direction, he winks at her. She looks at him and then at his clothes. She gets up in a huff and leaves.

"Give me a dollar," Willis says to him, holding out his hand.

"Why?" Tyrone asks.

Willis gives Tyrone a look that could kill. Tyrone produces a wrinkled dollar bill. Willis reluctantly takes it, opens the cash register and removes five twenty dollar bills and places the cash on the bar.

"Now I need you to finish your drink and then leave," he tells Tyrone.

Tyrone downs his drink. He's about to order another; Willis turns away and points to the exit.

Unloading

An unmarked van parks at the curb, it's early dawn, and the sun is cresting over the horizon. A side door slides open, and Ada looks up and down the area making sure the coast is clear. She leaps out onto the street; Zeke, in his black coat follows her; then Peter climbs out, puts on his coat. Dan grabs a shotgun after putting on his coat.

"We got everything?" Peter calls to Dan to check the van.

Dan looks in the back of the van before jumping out. Stone climbs from behind the wheel and looks up the block. People on the street stare at this group with their long black dusters blowing in the wind. Stone leads his crew; they march silently toward the Shelter.

They reach the Shelter to find a person by the name of Melvin and two thuggish drunks in the doorway, smoking weed.

One of them tells Stone, "Where do you think you're going?"

Stone throws back his coat, uncovers his revolver.

"Are you residents here?" Stone asks them.

"Hell no!" the other drunk tells him.

"I wouldn't live in a dump like this!" remarks the first one.

"You wouldn't live here, but you'd use this dump to smoke that shit, I think you two need to get out of here," Stone tells them.

The two thugs race off into the night. Melvin's about to follow them when Ada cocks the hammer of her gun and says to Melvin, "Get over there, I think you'll like the rooms here."

She cuffs him to a guardrail, giving Stone a reason to smile. Stone turns as he and his team charge into the building, stirring up a hornet's nest of commotion. There's screaming from the residents, both men and women; gunshots are going off alongside an exchange of return fire.

After thirty minutes or so, Stone's brother Glenn arrives with a support group of about twenty polices officers to assist Stone in the takeover.

Stone sees people scurrying in a panic for an exit. A handful of Glenn's officers in riot gear rush into the room and force the patrons to stand against the wall. Stone signals for some officers to cover the rear exit. He sees Glenn and gives him a nod, then goes about his business. The overhead lights are turned on, and Stones sees a trail of blood leading to an exit door. He draws his revolver and cautiously opens the door; a policeman follows him.

The exit leads down into a basement area with windows. Two gangsters are startled seeing Stone has his gun aimed at them. They throw their hands up.

The taller one lets out, "We ain't armed!"

The shorter man says, "We were just looking out the window …"

Stones catches sight of the taller man's bloody knuckles before he attempts to hide his hands in his pockets. Stones points to the hands and asks, "How did that happen?"

"I fell earlier in a rush to get down here," he tells Stone, "We're law-abiding citizens."

Just then an officer comes into the area with a man bleeding all over his face. The injured man points at the taller of the two and says in a garbled voice, "That's him, that's him. He's the one who beat me!"

"Are these the wise guys?" asks the officers. The man nods and passes out.

Stone calls to the other officer, "Take them in, see if they're wanted."

"Yes sir," says the officer, handcuffing both of them and escorting them out of the building.

Zeke has a list that he's writing in and checking off as he sits at the entrance to the Shelter. He looks at the women the police escort out of the building. He notices a man and woman who happened to be arm in arm. The man sees Zeke and pulls away from the woman; he heads for the side exit.

Zeke recognizes him as Edward Dennis; at least he looks vaguely familiar, a substance abuser in his forties; mandated to the Haven Shelter six months earlier according to Zeke's sheet. He's a resident with a three-year sentence pending on his completing the program.

He stops short when he sees an officer appear at the exit door. His girlfriend grabs his arm: she's

Daisey Golden, a part-time party girl in her thirties, still attractive, considering her lifestyle.

"We got to find a way out of here," Daisey squeals. She freezes looking around for another way out.

A policeman notices them looking desperate and says, "You two stay right there."

"Sir, we were just leaving," Daisey tells him.

Zeke notices Edward's jittery behavior and says, "What's your name?"

"Edward Dennis …"

Zeke checks his list and asks, "You live here?"

"I stay here now and then."

Zeke knows he's lying and tells him, "No one stays here now and then unless you're mandated to do so."

Zeke circles his name and shows him the list. He signals an officer to escort Edward into the building.

"Where are you taking him?" Daisey shouts.

Zeke pays Daisey no attention and tells the officer, "Take him, he's ours."

"Take me with him, I go where my man goes," Daisey claims, trying to follow them.

Ada grabs her arm. "Sorry, you can't do that, this a male facility."

Daisy does her best to keep track of Edward; then he disappears behind a closed door. Ada hands her off to another officer who takes her outside.

Stone comes upon a guard who appears

intoxicated. He seems to be about fifty or so; he has a drinking problem and should have been a resident rather than a guard.

"What's your name?" Stone asks him.

"Rufus Beck," he answers.

"Are you the guard for this facility?"

"Yes, I've been here for six years," Rufus tells him in a slurred speech.

"Get up," Stone orders him.

Rufus attempts to get out of the chair, but he can barely stand. Stone takes one quick whiff only to realize the man is soaking in alcohol.

Stone turns to the officers beside him, "Get him the hell out of here!"

They nod; Rufus tells them, "I can walk on my own." He almost falls into their arms.

"Are you going to be a problem?" an officer asks him.

They grab Rufus and drag him off.

Stone starts down the hall only to turn around and in disbelief sees a naked woman crawl out from under the table. She's also drunk.

"Where are my clothes?" she requests.

Stone grows furious. "I want every woman taken off this premises … Right NOW!" he yells.

A female officer covers the woman with a sheet, then accompanies her out of the building.

While officers and Stone's team sort out folks in

the recreation room, two gunshots ring out in another part of the shelter. Stone with his revolver drawn cautiously heads in the direction of the shots. Zeke, Peter and a few other officers follow him.

Stone comes across two men in the middle of the hall, attempting to negotiate with two hookers.

"You heard them gunshots?" a hooker says.

"Fuck that! What we gonna do?" one of the men asks her.

"You got seventy-five dollars, a piece?" the other hooker asks.

"Damn, I don't want to own the pussy …" the other guy says.

"We ain't giving it away," the first hooker tells them.

The negotiators are startled, seeing Stone and all the hardware coming in their direction.

"Who the fuck are they?" one of them says.

Stone motions for Peter to end the party. Peter comes and grabs both women by the arms; one of them attempts to pull away. Peter tightens his hold on her.

"Honey, your party is over."

She slips away from with a snarl, "I can walk on my own."

Ada steps in with an arm lock, "I got this …" The hooker squeals from the pressure placed on her.

Ada grabs the arm of the other woman as Peter lets her go and she leads both of them to the exit.

One of the tricks notices Peter has a sawed-off

shotgun under his coat. He nudges his partner and tells Stone, "We were just leaving."

Both men run out of the building. Stone tries to see what it was that scared them; then he notices that Peter shotgun has been sawed off; he approaches him and asks, "Where did you get that?"

Peter shrugs, "A friend …"

"Well, just make sure he gets it back," Stone tells him.

Peter gives him a smile and a nod. "As soon as I introduce her to anyone who needs introducing."

They hear moans coming from a room. Zeke looks at Stone and says, "I'll take care of this;" as he heads down the hall with two officers at his side.

"I'll check out the rest of this floor; see if we can find where those shots came from," Peter tells Stone.

"You do that, but I don't want any of you working alone," Stone yells to him.

Ada steps up her pace and joins Peter.

Ada and Peter take the stairway to a gym. Things appear normal; however, the moment Ada and Peter walk through the door a fist slams into her left cheek, knocking her onto the floor while someone breaks a chair over Pete's back, sending him flying in one direction and his sawed-off shotgun in another.

Ada rolls with the blow and quickly recovers to her feet, only to hear laughter and see a gun in her face. She quickly counters and subdues the assailant, leaving him out cold on the floor. Another thug charges her with a knife, she evades him, and knocks some of his teeth out with a roundhouse kick to the face. A third assailant, near Peter, pulls out a gun and raises it at Ada. Peter quickly rolls over and grabs his weapon and blows the man's kneecap off. The man goes down, dropping his gun.

Ada gives Peter a casual salute as he gets up. He tells her, "I knew this little lady would meet someone today." He gives his sawed-off shotgun a little kiss.

"Let's get these assholes downstairs," Ada tells him. Peter nods and pulls out the cuffs.

Combing through the second floor, they come to realize the walls have holes. The corridor's a mess with beer cans and bottles all over the floor. There are two residents, who are unaware that the NYPD is taking over the shelter, sitting in a doorway passing a bottle of beer to each other. Stone and his officers, sneak up on the floor.

A drunken resident turns and is surprised by Stone. He pulls out his knife and lunges forward. Stone blocks his thrust, throws an uppercut, then a hook. The guy goes down. The fight is over. A woman in her panties runs out of a room; a man in his underwear chases her. They see police and run back into the room.

A resident cries out, "Who are these guys?"

Zeke races onto the floor with a squad of uniformed police officers searching every room, asking anyone questions.

He finds a room with two men in it.

"Are you a resident in this program?" Zeke asks one man.

"The courts are deciding if they should put me in this program," he tells Zeke.

"Get your stuff, your stay here is over," orders Zeke.

"We didn't do anything," the other man says.

"Where's your room," Zeke asks him.

He points, "Down there, room four."

Zeke tells him to sit outside his door and remain there.

Stone walks onto the floor loudly yelling, "I want all residents to stand by your door.

Ada comes up and joins him. Stone notices a bruise on her chick. She realizes he sees it, but she waves off his concern by saying, "It's nothing." She goes ahead of him going from room to room looking for females.

Ada is yelling as she goes, "All you women in the rooms, you can leave. Right now! If I come and find you, you're going to jail!"

Women race pass Ada with their clothes in hand.

Again, Stone yells out, "All residents stand by your door!"

A team of officers goes in each resident's room. One officer brings a man out of a room wearing a robe while his partner follows them with a sword and shield. The second officer comes out of the room with an ax and a crossbow.

131

The first officer asks, "Who is this guy, Robin Hood?

His partner says, "He looks more like a chess piece."

Another officer pulls a man out of a room in his shorts and a shoulder holster; he's wearing a bulletproof vest. The cop behind them brings out two shotguns.

One officer exits a room with a half-naked man and a half-filled plastic bag of cocaine.

"We hit the jackpot!" the officer says.

"That's not mine!" claims the half-naked man.

"It was in your room," the officer says.

"I rent that room."

Stone walks up to him, "From whom?"

"Dennis, something … I don't know last names.

Stone tells the officer to hold him until they find this Dennis.

Two officers escort the man away.

They continue searching the second floor and go through the swinging doors to the other half of the floor. The place resembles a crack house, thick smoke drifts from room to room, out on into the corridor. A woman in her panties, races from one room into another as a man in his underwear chases her. He chases her, and they go into a lip lock.

Stone waits for his brother Glenn to join him with a few extra cops at his side. They move in on their suspects without being noticed.

"On my signal," Glenn tells Stone, who nods in agreement.

"I can see that this entire floor is going to jail," says Ada as everyone draws their weapons.

They rush into every remaining room on the floor. The police find a few women in the rooms, and they're escorted out of the building. All non-residents are escorted out of the building as well. The party's over.

Dan moves over to Stone's side and asks him, "Where do we go from here?"

"To visit my new office," Stone tells him, walking down the hall to the doorway.

Dan follows him.

School Daze

While Stone and his crew were finishing up their raid on the Haven Shelter, across town a school bus is traveling through the streets of the city. There's a bunch of boys singing in the rear of the bus; among them is Franklin Stone, Stone's son, and his best friend, Blake. The keep singing until they forget the words and most of them start mumbling a few lines of a verse that is total nonsense, causing all of them to break out into laughter.

They jokingly take jabs at each other over their ridiculousness.

"You coming over this weekend?" Blake asks Franklin.

"I can't; I'll be with my dad," Franklin tells him as his giggling subsides.

"That's good, your dad is cool," Blake laughs, giving Franklin a high five.

The group goes back to singing the verse of another popular song.

Some blocks away, Yat, the crackhead, nervously scans the street. He has his foot lightly on the pedal, ready at a moment's notice to take off. He watches the rear view-mirror and sees two masked, gunmen back out of a corner candy store; they jump into the back of the car. Once inside, Yat peels off, racing on into traffic.

The two men silently go through the stolen money; Yat takes a glance at them in the rear-view mirror.

"How did we do?" he shouts.

Yat barely avoids hitting a pedestrian, as the car swerves around a corner. There's the sound of a siren not too far away. Yat increases his speed, all the while, glancing at the rear-view mirror.

The sound of the siren increases as two police cars are gaining on Yat's car. Yat goes faster.

The school bus with Franklin and his schoolmates turns the corner at the same time as the car comes flying up the street. The car slams into the side of the bus, pinning it against a truck.

Everyone at the scene of the accident pays little attention to the car as the two men jump out of the car, discarding their masks. They make a quick effort to disappear amongst the crowd. Yat climbs out of the car, wiping his bloody face with his shirt tail. He stumbles around a corner.

Farther up the street pedestrians are yelling and racing toward the scene of the accident to offer what assistance they can.

"Get those children out of there!" screams one lady.

"Oh God, please help those children!" yells someone else.

Inside the bus are the screams of panicking children as smoke and sparks crackle loudly under the bus.

A police car pulls up, they see the school bus wedged between a car and a truck while people are attempting to pry open the front door.

One officer gets on the radio, "Dispatch, we have a 911 emergency. There's a fire beginning to engulf a school bus with children."

"Any need for medical assistance?" the dispatcher inquires.

"Of course, didn't you hear me. There are about twenty children trapped on the bus!" he barked.

"Yes, I'm relaying your request. Hang in there …"

The hood of the bus is blown off. The driver is unconscious. A few of the older kids race toward the back of the bus, knocking over kids and trampling some of them. Franklin and a few of the smaller kids crawl toward the back of the bus. Franklin realizes Blake's trapped between a steel bar and his chair. Franklin does his best to turn around, but he can't get past the other kids racing to the bus's rear.

A cloud of smoke quickly fills the bus as more sparks fly from a loose wire under the bus and gas spills from a busted hose. As the smoke intensifies the screams of the children grow louder, among them, Blake yells, "Get me out of here!"

Franklin is also yelling for help.

Sirens are heard approaching as one officer shouts, "We have to get those kids out of there!"

Upon arrival, firefighters rush to the scene and douse the fire. They use the jars of life to reach the driver, taking him out on a stretcher. There's still a lot of smoke; other police officials push the crowd of onlookers back so they can deal with the situation.

They quickly break open the back-escape exit and climb in, passing to the other waiting firefighters and paramedics the injured children, one by one.

The Director

Stone and Dan go up another landing to find the Director's Office. They tap on the door and enter only to find the place looks like a storage room. Cigarette smoke rings circle the room. Staff pictures, during better times, are on the wall. Files are carelessly stacked all around the room.

Their entrance startles a frightened, little man who jumps up on his feet and quickly puts on his bifocals while doing his best to straighten his old, worn jacket.

He's Rory Anderson, late fifties, working at the Shelter for over thirty years, looking as worn as the Shelter itself. He adjusts his glasses to see who is entering.

Rory nervously asks, "Can I help you? I don't think the meeting was scheduled for today, right?"

Stone waves away some smoke as Dan does the same.

"Mr. Anderson?" Stone asks.

Mr. Anderson is so frightened that he doesn't move. Dan takes some boxes off of two chairs.

Rory looks around nervously gathering some possessions, "I don't want any trouble, I was just leaving."

"Who do you think we are?" Stone asks him.

"Your men made it clear, yesterday. And with all the noise and ruckus going on out there, I'd just assumed you were carrying out your threat."

"My name is John Stone. I'm here from The Mayor's office," Stone says, then pointing to Dan, "This is Mr. …"

"Dan, just call me Dan," Dan says, offering a hand.

"Rory's confused, "You're from The Mayor's Office?"

"Yes," Stone tells him.

Stone assesses the room and goes over to the wall where pictures hang. He notices a photo of a Resident and Staff Cookout. Lloyd Harvey's dressed in a chef's uniform and stationed at the grill. Stone recognizes him as the slain victim from a police photo.

"Who's the cook?" Stone asks Rory.

Rory thinks for a moment, making sure of the person in the photograph.

"He was a friend," Rory says.

"Was?" Stone questions.

"He disappeared a few days ago," Rory explains.

"You don't think he just got up and moved on, do you?" Stone asks.

Rory begins to feel a little more at ease with Stone and Dan in the room. He moves closer to Stone and the picture, telling Stone, "He and I have battled with drug dealers and gangsters for the last twenty years. He never missed a day.'

"Had you filed a missing person report?" Stone asks.

"Those people have friends; I don't want to wind up missing too."

"Why didn't you bring in the police?" Dan asks.

"I called, and I got this," Rory says, pointing to a gash on the side of his face and continuing, "as my reward."

The phone in Anderson's office rings, Rory takes it.

"The Haven Shelter, Anderson speaking."

"Hello Anderson, it's Dr. Fairgood is John Stone there?"

"Hello, Dr. Fairgood. Yes, sir, he's right here," Rory says passing the phone to Stone.

"Stone here …"

"Stone, your son's been in an accident. He was taken to the (name of hospital) hospital," Fairgood tells him.

Stone gives the phone back to Rory and heads for the door.

He tells Rory, "I've got an emergency, you can brief my staff members."

"Was today supposed to be my last day?" Rory quickly asks Stone.

"We'll talk in the morning," Stone says exiting the room.

E.R.

Along with the usual array of patients in the emergency room; it has grown crowded with an influx of injured children from the bus crash hours earlier. There are new arrivals in wheelchairs and some other kids are on stretchers lined against the wall waiting for nursing attendants — Franklin's laid out on a stretcher. He's out cold. A nurse checks his vitals; she waves for an orderly.

"Take him to the third floor," she tells the orderly.

The orderly rushes Franklin pass a crowd of patients and fits him on a crowded elevator. The routine seems to go on without missing a beat as more paramedics continue bringing in more patients.

It's in the afternoon, and the sun is beginning to set in the horizon by the time Stone enters the emergency room at the hospital. He sees the place is crowded, stops an orderly and says, "I'm looking for my son."

"You'll have to check with the head nurse. She has a list of names," the orderly tells him.

"Where do I find her?"

The orderly turns around looking pass a sea of bodies and sees her near the entrance.

He points and says, "She's over there, near the entrance."

Stone sees her treating a patient's injuries. He works his way over to her, and when she's free, he touches her arm.

"I'm looking from my son, Franklin Stone. He came in this afternoon," he tells her.

"What kind of injury did he sustain?" she asks him.

"I don't know. I just heard my son was in an accident."

The nurse starts going through her list but is momentarily pulled away by the cries of a patient near her.

She has to put the list down momentarily to help the patient, Stone see Franklin's friend, Blake. Blake's against the wall on a stretcher. He sees Stone and waves to him.

Stone sees Blake and goes to him hoping for a quicker answer.

Blake tells him, "The car ran into our bus …"

"Blake, are you hurt?" Stone asks, relieved to see Blake.

"No, not really, my arm is a little sore."

"Where's Franklin, have you seen him?"

A nearby nurse overhears their conversation and asks, "Your last name's Stone?"

Stone nods.

"Your son is on the third floor. Come with me I'll show you the way," she says leading him. Before going, Stone turns to Blake, 'Blake, I'll call your parents and make sure they know."

"Thank you, Mr. Stone," Blake thanks him.

When Stone finally reaches his son's room he finds Victoria, his soon-to-be ex-wife, in the arms of Harold, her boyfriend, in the room. Harold's doing his best to offer her comfort as tears run down her face. They're startled to see Stone; he stops short at seeing them. Then he looks at his unconscious son in bandages, his heart sinks.

Victoria sees him and nudges Harold away, enough to get out of his embrace and charge at Stone; her eyes inflamed. When she reaches him, she jabs her finger in his face and spits out, "This is all your fault, damn you!"

She turns and grabs her belongings and storms out of the room with Harold in tow; he looks at Stone, not knowing what to say.

Stone is somewhat dismayed, but at this point and time; he couldn't give a rat's ass what Victoria thought of him. His only concern was his son. Stone quietly takes a seat in the chair nearest to his boy and watches him as he sleeps.

All in a Day's Work

Stone's vehicle pulls up at the front gate of the Haven Shelter in a sunny but windy morning. He sees an officer by the gate and salutes him.

"Good morning, sir."

"Good morning, officer," Stone returns the salutation.

Stone pushes his tired body into the building. He had stayed pass visiting hours at the hospital with Franklin until his son's health improved from the smoke inhalation.

As he enters his office, he finds Dan seating on the sofa amidst boxes, reading a newspaper, and Rory seated behind his desk. Rory and Dan greet him. Dan puts his paper down and gets up on his feet awaiting any further orders.

"Everything alright?" Rory asks Stone.

Stone nods. "Everything is fine," he says and then, without missing a beat, he picks up from where he left off, "How many residents are in the program?"

"It's hard to say," Rory tells him, "They show up whenever they want."

"Do you know any of them?"

"You don't get to know a person who shows up one day and not on the next," Rory explains.

Stone shakes his head and asks Rory, "What happen to your program?"

Rory stands up and begins collecting his things, "The neighborhood changed, we lost control of what the program was supposed to be."

Stone watches him, "Where do you go from here?"

Rory gives Stone a nervous smile, "I'm going to work with kids. I'd hope that would be a safer job."

Stone shakes Rory's hand in a sign of respect. "I wish you well."

"Thank you."

There's tapping on the door.

"Come in," both Rory and Stone say.

A man in a maintenance uniform enters. He's Ellis Harding, middle-aged, and the shy and silent type, as well as an ex-football player. He's a recovering heroin addict with nine years behind him of staying clean. Ellis stands where he entered and stares at the floor avoiding eye contact.

Rory introduces Ellis to Stone, "Ellis this is Mister Stone. He's taking my place."

Stone takes a step forward and offers his hand, saying, "I look forward to working with you."

Ellis remains quietly standing, staring at the floor.

Rory offers some assistance, and adds, "Mr. Stone will need you to keep the entire place clean and make this room look like an office."

Ellis nods in Rory's direction and leaves.

Dan asks Rory, "Does he talk?"

Rory gives Dan a nervous look saying, "He's quiet," then quickly adds, "but, he's a great worker."

The phone rings; Rory looks at Stone.

"It's your last day. You're still the Director.

Rory grabs the phone and answers, "Haven Shelter, Director Anderson speaking."

"Good morning, it's Deputy Mayor Dr. Fairgood. Is Director Stone there?"

"Yes, Sir," Rory answers passing the phone to Stone. "It's the Deputy Mayor."

"Hello," Stone answers.

"How's your son?"

"He suffered some smoke inhalation and still has some minor bruising, but other than that he's ok."

"You could've taken some time off," Dr. Fairgood tells Stone.

"Well there's quite a bit of work that needs to be done," Stone says.

"When will you start the program?"

Stone watches Rory ease out of the office and resumes his conversation with Fairgood, "The miracle starts tomorrow."

"Call if you need anything,"

"I will." Stone hangs up the phone and asks Dan, "Where's Zeke and everyone?"

"They should've finished up by now. They're probably downstairs in the front."

"Well let's go down and see what's what," Stone says, holding the door open for Dan.

Stone and Dan find Glenn, Zeke, Ada, Peter, and a few other officers plopped down on the steps of the building; they appeared exhausted.

He hugs his brother who was finally getting a chance to talk to Ada, turns to everyone saying, "Great job guys, thanks."

He touches his sister, Ada, on the shoulder and nods a thank you.

"The Lord helped us on this one," she says.

"What else could be in store for us?" Dan says, standing behind Stone.

Stone looks up and notices a long, black limousine easing up the street and stowing by the gate entrance.

It crawls to a stop, the rear window rolls down – it's Cory. Cory blows a puff of cigar smoke out of the window while smirking at Stone.

Stone sees Cory's patch; he points to his eye, mouthing the words to Cory, "What happened to your eye?" and smiles.

Cory becomes frustrated, taps on the divider to his driver, "Get me the hell out of here."

Stone watches the limo drive off. He's aware of the fact that this is not over.

Zeke, who was watching, stands and tells Stone, "We're going to need the Lord's help to run this place."

Stone nods while smiling at the departure of the

limo, "Yeah, we got a lot of work to do, but this is our house now, and I intend to keep it that way. No more Haven Shelter, it's the Haven House."

The others turned to him and nodded in agreement.

About the Authors

Joe Hunt, screenwriter actor, director, who studied drama at La Guardia Community College. He staged two plays. He graduated from City College of New York majoring in film making. Joe Hunt has been involved in almost every aspect of entertainment, from commercial photography to video as well as film and TV production.

Joe has four screenplays, one teleplay and a number of other stories to tell, however, this story, along with the series, is the most notorious he's ever told.

Amurá Oñaā is a new author, who is enjoying the creative process. Among the works written are a poem called "The Promise," a series of 300-word shorts entitled "The Amurati," and two novels - "The Seed (Origin of AI)," and "Jonathan Hood in Close the Door Behind You."

He is also a poet, songwriter, musician and sculptor, living in the City of New York.